C000057946

TRUE TO TYPE

*A collection of short stories
by journalists in
The Irish Times*

Dedicated to the memory
of our late colleague,
The Reverend Stephen Hilliard

All proceeds from the sale of this book are being donated to
The Reverend Stephen Hilliard Trust Fund

TRUE TO TYPE

*A collection of short stories
by journalists in
The Irish Times*

IRISH TIMES BOOKS
AND
SUGARLOAF PUBLICATIONS

First published December 1991
by
IRISH TIMES BOOKS
11-15 D'Olier Street, Dublin
and
SUGARLOAF PUBLICATIONS

ISBN 0 907011 18 7

Editor: Fergus Brogan
Title: Michael Cunningham
Cover design: Jarlath Hayes
Computer assistance: Joan Scales and Clare O'Connor
Project co-ordination: Brenda McNiff
Distribution: Irish Times General Services
Telephone (01) 6792022 ext. 309
Printed in the Republic of Ireland by Colour Books, Dublin

INTRODUCTION

NOT all journalists are hard chaws who shrug off their trenchcoats, pitch their hats onto a lurching hat-stand and bark out something about holding the front page.

The only person I've heard say anything of the sort was far from being a hard chaw. I don't think she owned a hat. The pub she was in had gone on fire; and she didn't so much bark as squeak. She was new to the job.

Stephen Hilliard, who couldn't stand cliche or its near neighbours cant and pretence, enjoyed the story. And that other one about Dean Inge who, abandoning St Paul's for Fleet Street, ceased to be a pillar of the Church to become a column in *The Times*. Stephen reversed the order and retained the admiration of his journalistic colleagues who made up this collection: an affectionate tribute from secret springs.

But "secret springs"? – Of Maeve Binchy, who once bore a touching resemblance to that reporter in the pub? Or Martyn Turner who strolls through life touching raw nerves in the sly and mighty? Declan Burke-Kennedy too is a novelist; Deaglán de Bréadún and Mary Morrissy are winning praise for their short stories. And Noel McFarlane's novel and movie about Ballyfermot were written before the North Side of Dublin started to look into its urban heart.

What these contributors have in common and share with the book's editor Fergus Brogan, and the others, is a working life in journalism, most of it spent in *The Irish Times*. Laid end to end they form an erratic line from Dublin to Moscow by way of Chicago and Belfast; and they wouldn't recognise a hat-stand if it slowly toppled over and fell on them.

The Irish Times has a long history of harbouring writers of fiction, from Myles na Gopaleen to Benedict Kiely. Someone on the staff once unravelled "The Mystery of Edwin Drood". The editor lost the script and the author was compensated with a small but steady income for life. We should all have paid more attention to the journalist Dickens.

Now life has not only imitated art but so far outstripped imagination that the everyday work of journalism has a ring of fiction and the most straightforward account of events an innocent touch of satire: "Man Bites Dog" trotting after reality.

In the circumstances, "True to Type" is an antidote, a hint of light – if not entirely comic – relief for darkish times. You will find the latest disasters in the usual place; this is for later. Hold on to your copy; no home should be without one.

Dick Walsh

CONTENTS

The Wrong Caption	*Maeve Binchy*	9
Document No 2	*Joe Culley*	16
The Tiger and Pink Gin	*Mary Cummins*	23
Lucky Singing	*Noel McFarlane*	33
Thirty-six by Thirty-six	*Arthur Reynolds*	42
Leonie	*Declan Burke-Kennedy*	45
Saturdays	*Mary Maher*	61
Tara Streete Tayles Drawings	*Seamus Martin Martyn Turner*	64
Air on a G-String	*Kieran Fagan*	77
Ending It	*Padraig O'Morain*	86
Space Invader	*Fergus Brogan*	93
The Cantilever Principle	*Mary Morrissy*	97
White Space	*Deaglán de Bréadún*	104
Striking Hours	*Paddy Woodworth*	109
The Baby Carriage	*Eugene McEldowney*	122
Forget the Front Page	*Tom Glennon*	127
In Prosperity and Adversity	*Pat Comerford*	132
The Great Trek of Willem Louren	*Seamus Martin*	138
Art, Poetry, Music and Money	*Brendan Glacken*	146

© 1991 The Authors

All rights reserved. No part of this book may be reproduced
or utilised in any form or by any means, electronic or me-
chanical, including photography, filming, recording, video
recording, photocopying or by any information storage and
retrieval system, or shall not, by way of trade or otherwise be
lent, resold or otherwise circulated in any form of binding or
cover other than that in which it is published, without prior
permission in writing from the publishers. The moral rights
of the authors have been asserted.

THE WRONG CAPTION

Maeve Binchy

NORA had once worked on a paper where they printed a picture of a couple's golden wedding anniversary with the caption "Don't know why but *must* get in, apparently he's a big party supporter". The paper had been a collector's item, heads had rolled and nobody ever wrote down any instruction that could not be printed as it stood.

The next paper she went to believed wrongly that its editor was a charismatic and so the front pages were filled with pictures of arm-waving congregations. It was only when the editor was heard to say that the best caption for the twentieth such picture should be "Jesus, not again" that people realised they had misinterpreted his allegiances. But not soon enough to alert those who thought that "Jesus, not again" was exactly the three-word snappy line they needed under the picture and printed it.

So by the time she had made it to a national daily, Nora was only too well aware of the dangers of the wrong caption. She was almost paranoid about scraps of paper with any misleading information on them being left around the place. The others laughed at her. They tried to tell her that she was in the big time now not in a Mickey Mouse, hicksville weekly paper. But Nora said that mistakes could happen anywhere, and that if you had lived through the misery of that couple whose golden wedding was destroyed by the reference to their political clout you too would be careful. If you had been part of the team that dealt with the hurt telephone calls and letters over the seemingly blasphemous caption to a picture of

9

innocent worshippers then you would regard caution as your watchword.

Nora had other watchwords too. She was uncompromisingly honest. Her weekly expenses could never have been criticised by the harshest of auditors, nor referred to as splendid fiction like so many of other journalists might have been. Whenever she was sent to cover a rally or demonstration, Nora made a huge and concentrated effort to count the number who turned up rather than accept the word of authorities who usually said there was a trickle of protest and the organisers who said it was a seething multitude.

She would not write glowing pieces about the magical quality of some free cosmetic, she never praised a hotel that gave her a free lunch and hinted at a free weekend. She didn't butter up those in high places who might have the power to give her a better job, a brighter window to sit at, a bigger by-line. Everyone on the paper liked Nora, they accepted her obsession with getting the right caption as a kind of nervous tic, like the way some people had to have an undrunk cup of coffee growing cold on their desk before they could begin to type a story, and others kept saying "you know what I mean" after every sentence.

And as the years went by men being men said to each other that it was strange Nora hadn't married, she was quite a nice looking girl. Not bad at all, they would say with some surprise and shake their heads. The only criterion for getting married was being nice looking so if Nora had passed that test wasn't it odd that she hadn't gone the distance.

And women being women used to say that Nora kept her private life to herself unless you asked her and if you did ask her she said like everyone else that all the good men were long gone and had usually been nailed down by an appalling vixen.

Then Nora started mentioning Dan a bit.

Dan was a teacher, she met him when she was doing an educational story, she had gone to his school with a photographer, and Dan had been impressed that Nora had checked the names of those posing for the group photograph herself. She had her notebook out and confirmed their names, left to right writing everything down.

"I thought the photographer did that" Dan said. "On normal markings we do"; the photographer was easy-going and resigned. He explained that in the paper they were all used to Nora. She was a cross to bear. In all other ways she was normal. Everyone was allowed one obsession.

Dan thought she was delightful, the way she blew her hair out of her eyes, and her pencil flew across her notebook in the hiero-glyphics of shorthand.

"I didn't think people still used that" he said as they walked in easy conversation through the school grounds.

"Only ancient ones like myself do" Nora confessed. "It's from the era of belted raincoats, and hold the front page. You wouldn't remember that."

"I'm as old as you are" Dan said stung.

"I'm nearly forty" Nora said.

"I'm thirty-six and a half" said Dan.

It was the real thing. More real than anyone in the office had ever known. Nora began to lose weight and talk to the youngsters about how many calories there were in so-called low-fat yoghurt. She took serious advice on hair colour and opted for highlights. She ex-amined her clothes critically, she said she didn't want to be palmed off with useless comforting things like fashion being what you chose to wear, what you felt comfortable in. She said she didn't give a damn about comfort, she wanted to be stylish and fast.

She was certainly reading informative literature about cosmetic surgery if perhaps falling short of the final commitment. But she said these were desperate times, she was going to meet Dan's mother and didn't want to look older than her.

"She could hardly have conceived at the age of two or three" Nora's friend Annie said, but Nora took no notice whatsoever of Annie who had married, unwisely as it turned out, but at the age of twenty-one and had no need for rejuvenation in the high passion of her courting.

At Dan's mother's house Nora made thirty-seven ageist jokes putting herself down. She mentioned cradle snatching seven times and said she had never really got used to the Talkies, and she found more peace in black-and-white movies, technicolour hurt her eyes. To Dan's bewildered mother Nora pretended that she had done her early reporting during the First World War and had cut her teeth on the Suffragette movement.

On the way home, Dan stopped the car and asked her to marry

him. "You're too young, you don't know your own mind" Nora said.

"In the forty or fifty good years we may have ahead of us, it would be a huge relief to me if you didn't have to keep this up the whole time" Dan said.

"Will they be good years?" Nora hardly dared to believe it.

"I think they will if we could drop the geriatric patter." Dan was thoughtful. "I can see you interrupting my speech on our wedding day with a few references to weddings you remember with the Tsars or maybe if it's a bad day you might go back to the Brehon Laws". "Wedding?" Nora cried. "You mean a wedding with people looking at us?" "No, no" Dan reassured her, "there will be nothing like that, there will be instructions on the invitation that they are to arrive blindfolded".

They fixed on a day only two months ahead. Nora opened her mouth to say that at her age every minute counted if you were to beat the sell-by date but she remembered what Dan had said, so she didn't say it.

Nora gave herself only one hour a day to talk about her wedding plans, she was worried that her work was suffering because she thought so much about Dan with love and hope, and about the wedding day with dread.

Annie was mystified. "It's only a day for god's sake, you look great for god's sake, what on earth is worrying you?"

"If you could point me to a shop which says 'Everything for the Ageing Bride' then maybe I'd calm down." Nora's face looked tragic. The girls in the office directed Nora to the trendy boutiques. They told her to shut up or they wouldn't organise an office collection for her.

She had to sneak time off to tour the boutiques. They were all staffed by eleven-year olds. She found herself apologising and backing out. "Only having a look" she would squeak looking like a shop-lifter.

Eventually she realised she would have to come to some decision, the day was drawing nearer and she had reached no conclusion since she had had no conversations let alone fittings in these frightening places.

"I'm looking for something for a wedding" she said eventually in a high shrill voice unlike her own.

The young assistant seemed to look at her as if it was a very gross suggestion.

"A wedding?" she repeated doubtfully.

Nora had only promised to stop wise-cracking about age to Dan, there had been no undertaking that she could not make such pleasantries when she was not in his company.

"Not strictly a mother-of-the-bride outfit, but I do have a key role so it needs to be smart" she said. "Friend of your daughters, is it?" the eighteen-year old was trying to be helpful. Nora's heart was like lead.

It was of course a nightmare, they kept asking her what the bride was wearing, she kept saying she didn't know. She had now announced that she was going to be matron of honour, and the bride was her dearest friend.

"Why don't you ask her what she's wearing?" asked the increasingly confused assistants.

"I don't like to ask" said poor Nora piteously.

They wanted to know if the bride would be wearing white, Nora had poured scorn on that one.

"It's a pity" said the boutique manager" if she *were* wearing white you could have worn anything."

"I think she'll were white if I ask her to" Nora said desperately.

They found this a truly confusing wedding but they kitted her out incredibly well considering they had been given absolutely no information and a dozen contradictory signals. The dress and hat were stunning.

"I think you'll outshine the bride entirely" said the boutique manager.

"Ah to hell with the bride" said Nora and saw that they took rather a long time to verify her credit card. She didn't blame them for assuming she was barking mad. It would have been the only reasonable explanation.

She collected the dress, and the hat and the shoes the day before the wedding. They all stood around admiring her.

"What kind of a bag will you have?" they asked.

Nora had forgotten the bloody bag, she couldn't carry her huge office shoulder bag, any evening bags she had at home would be wrong. There was nothing in the shop that suited, one of the assistants lent hers.

"You can drop it in the day after" she said generously.

Nora opened her mouth to say she would be on her honeymoon and closed it. Anyway Annie could leave it back for her.

The day was a blur. Dan's mother who had been keeping her distance a bit after the first startling meeting was full of praise.

"You look absolutely lovely" she said.

Nora had a remark ready about the picture of Dorian Gray in her attic but bit it back. Her colleagues praised her to the hilt, they had even arranged to have a wedding picture in tomorrow's paper. Nora was about to help the photographer set it up.

"I can do it Nora" he said, "there's only two of you, I can write the caption."

And as she looked at the way Dan was watching her, she smiled, her first real smile of the day. It was going to be great, forty or fifty years maybe, it was something she never thought would happen to her. She sighed a deep sigh of happiness.

Annie took the bag back to the boutique the next day. They were agog in the shop. They had seen the photo in the paper.

"She married him herself" said the boutique manager in outrage. "I knew there was something fishy about it all, she said to hell with the bride, nobody with any feeling would have said that." Annie hadn't an idea what they were talking about, but she could trust Nora to have got mixed up in a shop where everyone was mad.

"Was there a scene in the church you know, like Jane Eyre?" asked the girl who looked as if she should still have been at school. Annie was dying to be out of the place, she had a hangover and a nineteen-year-old unsatisfactory marriage to worry about.

"No, no scenes" she said tersely.

"Didn't they have to read new bans or anything?" These assistants were beginning to doubt that the institution of marriage could survive with people like Nora around.

Annie began to think that her head was worse than she suspected, she started to leave the shop.

"Is that why she didn't come back herself, she's actually gone off with him?" they asked.

"Of course she's gone off with him, on her honeymoon."

The baby-faced manager was a liberated woman, she said she always liked to see women be assertive but this was ridiculous. "You should not be assertive at the expense of a sister" she said. "My one hope when I saw the picture was that they had written the wrong caption."

Annie knew that she now needed both a cure and an appointment with an analyst. With all the strength she could muster she said "It was *not* the wrong caption. Whatever mistakes Nora made in her life and she made many including choosing this place to buy her wedding outfit, she was never responsible for a wrong caption in her life."

She left unsteadily watched by the staff of the boutique.

"Do you think she was the one who was meant to be the bride?" one of them said as they saw Annie teetering away.

It was a mystery. Like all young people they hated mysteries and were put out about it for a very long time.

Document No 2

Joe Culley

THE last thing Ciana expected to find floating in the fountain was a body. Not just 'a body', but more specifically a corpse, a human one. An empty crisps bag, yes, perhaps even – given the times that were in it – a condom or two; these things one might expect to find in the fountain.

But not a corpse. Ciana (BA His. H.Dip UCD) was certain Lutyens hadn't put him there. In fact, he hadn't been there last Saturday. Then, like today, Ciana had been so alone in the park she entertained herself by pretending to be the last woman on earth, waiting for her lover the last man, who would be either Gabriel Byrne or Cardinal O Fiaich, God forgive her. No, Lutyens wasn't responsible for this particular corpse. The war memorial was a masterpiece of geometric symmetry, all lines and triangles and circles positioned in perfect balance. Ciana understood this instinctively, and sensed that if Lutyens had placed a corpse in this fountain, then he would have placed a corpse in its mirror fountain as well, and Ciana could see from where she stood that he hadn't.

She was certain too that the corpse was a he. A rather handsome he at that, probably not much younger than herself, mid-twenties somewhere. The corpse had (or 'had had' – it's always difficult to know which tense to use with a dead man) a strong chin with just the hint of a cleft. The narrow mouth was formed by finely sculpted lips which had probably once been an arousing red but were now a more purple hue. The nose, Ciana knew, would be described properly as aquiline. The attractive little hump at its bridge was perfectly suited to propping up the Lennon glasses the corpse wore. From behind those lenses his oh-so-green eyes stared out with a slightly disconcerting light, but that might just have been a trick of the sun's reflection.

Yes, it was a handsome face, marred only by the hole, about half an inch in diameter, in the exact centre of his forehead. It had been made, Ciana was certain, by a .22 bullet. Well, no, Ciana wasn't *certain* it was a .22, but she thought Elmore Leonard was brilliant and she knew that if whoever had shot the corpse had used a .44 Magnum or something like it then she wouldn't have been given the chance to admire the handsome face.

The really appealing thing about the dead man was the uniform. Ciana had a 'thing' about uniformed men, gardaí, bus drivers, postmen and – Lord bless us and save us – priests. This corpse was dressed more like some army bloke, though which army Ciana wasn't certain. Although well preserved, even fresh, he had a sort of old timey feel about him, as if he belonged in a photograph of someone's grandfather.

Nor was it entirely accurate to say he 'floated' in the fountain. More like he was just resting. He lay on his back, submerged to his breast pockets, his toe-caps surfacing like little black icebergs. But his left arm draped rather casually over the fountain's rim and his head seemed cushioned there. In fact, at that moment it seemed to Ciana that he was actually...but no, that's ridiculous, dead men don't, can't...Despite herself, she turned her head to follow his 'gaze'. A jet already too high to distinguish the airline, was banking southeast over the Phoenix Park, belly reflecting the early after-noon sun.

"Were you ever up in one of them yokes?"

O Christ. O sweet suffering Jesus Christ.

"Did you hear me love? I said were you ever up in one of them things?"

Ciana was trying to gauge the distance to the boathouse, think-ing she could make it provided he couldn't fly as well as speak, deciding against it when she realised her legs would not move.

"Excuse me, missus. Am I boring you?" She turned back to him. The hole the slug had made was still there, he hadn't moved, his skin was still too pale.

"Ah, marvellous. I have your attention. Welcome back to the

land of the living. I said, I wonder were you ever above in one of them contraptions?"

This dead man is speaking to me without moving his lips, Ciana thought. I have been addressed by a dead ventriloquist. In a fountain.

"I was," Ciana mumbled.

"What's that? I'm sorry love, you'll have to speak up a small bit, the old hearing's not what it was."

Ciana cleared her throat. "I was, yes." Christ.

"Were you? Marvellous. I was never in one myself, never had the privilege, so to speak. Casement offered to bring me up once, but events sort of overtook us, you know?"

"I can imagine," Ciana replied. By God, she could imagine alright. Imagine meeting a chatty cadaver. Imagine sitting barefoot in your cell waiting for the doctor's monthly visit.

"Where was it you went?" he continued.

"Went when?" Finding it hard to concentrate.

"Went when, do you hear the girl. In the aeroplane. Where was it you went in the aeroplane?"

"London. We flew to London."

"London? Marvellous, an príomhchathair na Sasanaigh, a grand place, London. I was there myself in '21 with a few of the lads. Travelled over on the mail boat then of course. Did I ever tell you about our dinner with Lloyd George?"

"No, I don't believe you did." Suddenly Ciana realised that if she did not soon sit down, she would fall down. "Do you mind," she asked, gesturing toward the fountain.

"Of course, rest yourself, lig do scíth." She approached and sat sidesaddle on the rim, balancing with her left foot on the ground. His green eyes no longer held her. He lay slightly to her right, and she found she could close her eyes and raise her face to the sun without seeming impolite. There was little heat in the sun, but with eyes closed her imagination could animate this interlocutor. When he spoke, she pictured his moving lips, his gesticulations, the life signs he was so perverse to withhold.

"We were all over for the Treaty negotiations. Erskine was there, Barton, Gavan Duffy and MacBride – there was the boyo. Laugh? – Griffith and Collins too. He was one wet rag, Collins. He'd turn a wedding to a wake just walking through the door. And Erskine and Arthur could hardly be in the same room together.

"Anyways, one of the nights, in October I think it was, we were all due to dine with the Brits, Lloyd George, Churchill, Chamberlain, Birkenhead, the whole crew. Now, Charlie Duffy, Sean and myself had made an impromptu tour of several local hostelries earlier, and when we arrived in to Number 10, half an hour late, I was absolutely fluthered, ar meisce ar fad.

" When we were ushered into the dining hall we offered as they say fulsome apologies, but Collins caught me with his dark beady eyes and I swear to God he'd have shot me on the spot if he hadn't been a guest.

"We sat down to dinner finally anyway, and things were going along grand for a while until Big Mick tells the waiters not to provide me with any more wine, the bowsie. Well, that tore it. So I waited my chance, and when Winny let fly with some pompous drivel about the Empire, I stood up on my chair and announced to the assembly, 'Gentlemen, there is one place in the Empire where the sun never shines.' Then I snapped about face and dropped my trousers. I fell off the chair then and must have given the brain box a fair wallop because the next thing is I'm on the boat sailing home. Brugha met me at Kingstown and bought me a Midleton."

Ciana realised she was smiling. Again she turned to study her still companion. He continued to stare across the river. Ciana opened her mouth to speak, but stopped and quickly glanced about to see if anyone had arrived as he related his tale. Satisfied they were still alone, she inquired, "You were in the Army then? In the Free State with Michael Collins? That's your uniform?"

The uncommon silence from the dead man told Ciana she had got this one badly wrong, but before she could attempt a recovery he replied.

"I was in the Army, yes. The Republican Army. The Army of the one and true Poblacht na hEireann proclaimed outside the GPO on Easter Monday 1916 by the sainted Padraig Henry Pearse, the Army that remained loyal to our nation despite the base efforts of Collins and his Castle friends to divide the land, the Army..."

"Oh, please, my apologies, of course, I wasn't thinking," Ciana faltered. She needed to change the subject. As her mind worked furiously her eyes fixed on his facial blemish, and without proper consideration she blurted, "Did it hurt?"

"What's that? Did what hurt?"

"The, uh, your...accident. Your head..."

"My head? When I fell? Oh yes, I understand you now, tuigim anois. You mean my plug hole, where I got drilled. I forget it's there, you know, been so long."

"Did it hurt, your getting...drilled?"

"No, no, not a terrible lot, when I think about it. More of a shock, really. You get over it."

"Who shot you? I mean, if you don't mind my asking." Was he smiling?

"Dev."

"Dev? De Valera? You're joking."

"Dee Va Bloody Lera, the same man. The Spanish Changeling."

"Rubbish. I mean, I don't think Dev shot anyone in his entire life, not even at Boland's Mill."

"Now, you got that part right missus. He didn't have the magairlí for that sort of business, if you understand me. By God he did not. No, but he wasn't slow to *have* it done."

"But why? You were both anti-Treaty. Weren't you?"

"Did you ever notice that the lads who got the big jobs, de Valera and Sean T. and the like, were all as they say 'conspicuous by their absence' when we were fighting the Tans? The 'President' managed to keep terribly busy Stateside there, and O'Kelly had better French than he had Irish by the time he arrived home."

"Stop it. You're just playacting now. I'd say you're only jealous because you blew your chance of a Cabinet post with your loutish behaviour in London."

"You sound like my mother now, God be good to her. Loutish behaviour is it? Did you ever hear tell of Document No 2?"

"I did of course. Dev's alternative to the Treaty."

"Dev's alternative plan to sell out our northern comrades is what you mean girl. He let us down terribly there."

Christ, Ciana thought. My luck. I meet a man who has been dead for three generations and he turns out to be a crank. She stood and began to pace as he rabbitted on about sacred oaths and empty formulae, the Second Dáil, rifle grenades and some fella named Cope. She cut in.

"Listen, a lot of people didn't agree with Document No 2 but he didn't have them all shot for it."

"Ah well, I wasn't shot over the document exactly. Not entirely, that is."

"No?" He was smiling again.

"No. No, to tell the truth, I don't think Dev ever really forgave me for putting my tongue in his mouth." Now Ciana was smiling.

"You what?" Quietly.

"Well love, you have to understand, we were in prison at the time you see, Arbour Hill. You know what it's like for men in prison. You get...urges. Anyway, I did it for a dare as much as anything."

"A dare?"

"A dare, yeah. There was a whole crowd of us there up the Hill after the call to dump arms. So anyway, one afternoon we're all out in the yard, and Dev's over in the corner having a little confab with Austin Stack. Austin had just come off hunger strike, God bless him, and one of the lads gets this idea, thought it might cheer Austin up a bit."

"That you should kiss Dev."

"Sin é. So, I stroll across the yard, you see, and Austin sees me coming, and I give him a quick wink, even though he doesn't know the scéal. I go up to Dev, gabh mo leathscéal, a Uachtaráin, says I, then up on my toes and I plant a big wet póg on his gob."

"He was surprised."

"He was. And poor Austin, I thought he might die right there, he couldn't breathe. It was great gas."

"So Dev had you shot."

"He did. Not straight away, mind you."

"No, of course not," she said, with a slight sarcasm. "You were in prison, after all, weren't you?"

"We were."

"So when did they get you?"

"A clear, bright night in November – I remember there was a heavy frost. '26 it was. Or '27."

"You don't remember what year you were shot dead?"

"It was a long time ago. Fadó fadó. I was strolling into town along the quays, by the Four Courts, and this old Lancia like the Staters were still using pulls up alongside. These two latchicos jump out and 'invite' me to come along with them. They were armed, I wasn't. We came straight out here to Cosgrave's place."

"How do you know they were Dev's men?"

"Because, doubting Tomasina, as soon as we climb out of the car one of them says, 'The President would like you to have this', and BANG, that's all she wrote. I never opened my mouth."

"I'd say you opened your mouth once too often."

"Well yes, there is that, I suppose."

"This was '26 you say. Or '27?"

"Around then. As I said, it was a long..."

"But this place wasn't built until the late '30s. There was no fountain here in the '20s."

"Nor did I say there was, love. No, after they drilled me, they dumped me in the river. But I could get no rest at all down there, what with the crews splashing up and down all day and night. So I moved up here during the Emergency. During a blackout." Just then, he seemed to shift himself, though Ciana knew he *didn't* shift himself.

"But listen," he continued, "enough about me. What do you do yourself?"

"Me? Ah, you wouldn't be interested."

"I would. Go on, try me."

"Ah no. Sure, you'd be bored stiff."

THE TIGER AND PINK GIN

Mary Cummins

'TIGER, tiger, burning bright, in the forests of the night", Cas Jones incanted. She liked to be thought intellectual.

"No, No, NO", Lou Rees exploded. "It'll be TIGER, TIGERRR, BURRR-ning bright in the PITS, the pits of TIGER BAY". The words rolled off her tongue with energetic melody as she swivelled her big brown eyes and licked her red lips.

She appealed to Nora, pulling the last few rollers out of her bouncy hair. "Ah, come on, bach. It's the Royal Navy not just some old steamer".

"Are they still called tramps?" There was a bitchy edge to Cas Jones's voice. Long and slim, she lay the full length of Nora's bed, smoothing her silk wrapper from time to time.

"Just because you went to grammar school, Cas Jones", Sian Bates muttered. "There's no need to be so bloody snobby". She went on clipping her toe-nails and placing the cuttings neatly on a tissue.

Nora could sense the makings of a tired squabble. They were all worn out, aching. It was the end of another long, busy day. They had all come off duty at 8pm and straggled back to the nurses' home in ones and twos. Some went to watch television. Others went to steam in hot baths. Five of them were lying around Nora's room. Apart from Cass Jones they were still half in and out of their uniforms.

Lou Rees had put in her heated rollers after the phone call. She had answered it mechanically, expecting "Riveting Reg" as they all called him. He rang almost every night from Merthyr Tydfil. They had been going out since they were 14 and would get married in 18 months as soon as the finals were over.

It was not Riveting Reg. It was some sailors who were having a party on the Tiger. In the mirror Lou Rees arched one eyebrow pleadingly at Nora. "Come on bach...Flower?"

Nora's twanging nerves snapped. "No. And I mean no. This place is turning into a right brothel. They ring up from here, there and everywhere and expect a drove of us to amuse them. And more." She threw a vicious look around the room.

"Well, you see Nora, thank Calvin or Henry the whoever-it-was, we don't have to go to confession", Cas Jones said. Apparently airily, without looking up, pretending to pleat a ridge in the slippery, turquoise silk, she said: "Not that you'd have much to tell, would you, ducks?" There was malevolence under the dulcet tones.

"Nor you, Cas Jones", Sian Bates stormed. "Not much sins you'd have with that Mammy's boy from the tennis club. Not much you can do in the front seat of a sports car, is there?

"And has he asked you to meet his mam yet?" Sian Bates pursued relentlessly. This, they all knew was pushing the knife in. This was why they were all terrified when Sian Bates's sunny, joking, usual self, lost her rag.

"Well? Has he?"

"No", Cas Jones was quiet but recovered smoothly. "It's early days yet".

"And Nora has a medical student, anyway, hasn't she?" Sian Bates who was Nora's best friend, continued her barrage. "A cut above some kind of accountant or whatever he calls himself. Probably a jumped-up office boy..."

"He will be a chartered accountant", Cas Jones's modulated tones were rising to a shrill.

Libby Thomas giggled nervously. Susie Davies, pretty, blonde and buxom nodded ingratiatingly. Cas Jones was her ideal.

There was silence. Nora looked out the window. It was a crisp, early summer evening, still bright. "Mrs Morganstern died", she said to no-one in particular. They each knew the personalities and minutiae of each other's wards.

"Ah, love her". Lou Rees was quickly sympathetic. "And her husband and kiddies. Well, well, well." They were quiet.

"Twenty-to-eight it happened. Right in the middle of visitors.

But sister didn't get into a flap, wanting to have her laid out before nights came on. She was a Jew", Nora added.

"Great, isn't it?" Susie Davies looked on the bright side of everything. "They just come and take them away themselves".

"What do they do with them, I wonder?", Libby Thomas asked and Cas Jones was just beginning to tell her, raising herself on one elbow when Nora turned swiftly from the window.

"Well, come on then. Who's coming? What are we waiting for?"

They stared at her, baffled. They all knew how difficult it was to get Nora to go even to the doctors' res or on a blind date to please one of their boyfriends. But to a ship's party in the bay?

"Well, did you ever..." Cas Jones started to sing and then jumped to her feet when she saw Nora's face. "I'll get something dishy for you to wear", she gushed and fled.

Lou Rees was ecstatic. "I'm wearing my new blouse".

"With the elastic around the neck?", Sian Bates's voice was heavily censorious. "With all those bloody sailors. Are you out of your mind, girl?"

But Lou Rees was gone, dreading that Nora would change her mind.

"What will you wear?" Libby Thomas was curious.

"My green suit", Nora said firmly. She had bought it for her last holidays home. Her mother was always telling her she should always have one good thing.

"But for a party...?" Even Sian Davies was doubtful.

"Oh, for god almighty's sake, what is all the fuss about? A party is a party is a party. If it's good enough for the pub it's good enough for Tiger Bay."

"Tell Lou Rees I'll be ready in five minutes and to be down", she said firmly to Susie Davies, "and make sure to open the fire escape after night sister's rounds.

THE narrow streets down to the docks of Cardiff were dank, gloomy rivulets of narrow houses. Like the sinister settings of Jack the Ripper films. Nora was terrified. Even Lou Rees was muted by the smirk of the taxi driver when they said the docks.

They whispered the plans. If it was the dregs, Lou Rees would pretend to have an epileptic fit. She was good at that. She took out her small mirror for the umpteenth time and ruffled her curls out in a wider aureole around her face. Nora envied her big, brown eyes and long dark lashes. She watched her put on more lipstick.

The taxi bumped along, sometimes over cobbles. The darkness was pervasive, relieved by the dim streetlights. Some windows glimmered weakly behind mean curtains.

Suddenly there was a landscape of large warehouses. The streets widened out. Instantly, there was light streaming, beaming at them. They screwed up their eyes against the glare. It was coming from a blazing white ship that gleamed and shone out of the pitch blackness. The shining whiteness of the long and high boat would have been enough to blind them but from top to bottom, from stem to stern it was twinkling with bulbs strung along in lines, a massive Christmas tree on water.

"Ooh, look at that...look at THAT." There was awe in the taximan's voice.

"That's the Tiger, that is. On the telly it was. Wilson, damn his face, was on it, he was. With that bloke from Rhodesia. UDI and all that...Smith, that's who he was. Oh, there's a sight, boyo..." He warbled with excitement

There were other cars drawing up and leaving. Up on the deck Nora could see people moving around. Much activity. They paid the taximan who thanked them respectfully, "Give anything to go on that one, I would", he confided.

Within seconds it was all formal and unreal. A line of smartly-uniformed sailors were at either side of the gang-plank. An efficient, worried-looking officer rushed towards them. "From the Royal. Oh, goody. Follow me girls."

Lou Rees was trying to repress her giggles. Nora gave her a sharp shot on the shin. But she was just as nervous inside. She had expected some kind of drunken, sloppy affair at worst or aimless, good-humoured ejits like the ones at the tennis club, at best. Her only experience of a ship was the emigrant boat from Rosslare to Fishguard. She could never remember seeing a real sailor on it. Just crowds of grim women, cranky, vomiting kids, sad men and young people like herself, trying to keep a stony composure on their wobbly features.

At the top a tall, noble man shook their hands as if they were important. He was elegant in his navy uniform. His wife beside him wore an Oriental shawl over a long evening dress. She had scrappy grey hair and a beaky face. She looked them over and nodded frostily.

"Cow", muttered Lou Rees as they followed the frenzied young man down narrow steps and into a long, low room.

Uniformed men were everywhere; talking to each other, some were with smart-looking women. They were dressed in easy clothes. Nora could feel her face reddening with hot embarrassment. Her suit was tight and thick and clumsy. The other women looked graceful, relaxed. Even Lou Rees's adventurous blouse and bright skirt blended.

The voices were a well-bred, confidential murmur. Heads turned to look at them. A waiter with a silver tray of drinks was beside them.

Nora was adamant. She would not stay, she vowed. She could say she was sick. She could bully Lou Rees; tell her she'd tell Reg. She could lock herself in the toilets. Did they have toilets on a ship? God, god, damn, damn, damn.

"Ladies?" A slim young man was in front of them. He focused on Lou Rees. He was Rich – Rich Taylor. His teeth gleamed at them. He pushed long fingers through a slick of hair that fell back onto his forehead in seconds. There was a signet ring on his left small finger. A gold watch clasped his wrist below a fine, white cuff.

"Dentist, that's me. Ha? More or less your line girls, eh?"

He looked at the drinks tray. "No, no, Michael, old boy. It has to be pink gin. Or have all the old blimps swigged it all? No? Good man."

He was dashing, bronzed, charming. Every adjective that Nora had ever read in praise of men could be lavished on him. His laugh was a bit high but his Navy uniform was perfection, flattering his golden skin. Was he a young Cary Grant or an untortured Montgomery Clift, Nora wondered. He even flashed a gleam of teeth at her.

It did not help. If only he would pretend she was not there at all. Her skin was singing with puce pain. She felt large and cumbersome. Why didn't he just take Lou Rees off to dance? Then she could run.

"Ah, John, there you are fella. Come and meet these two lovely girls." He called over a man who had been talking to a group beside them. "You'll have to get this fella to dance", Rich winked at Nora and escaped with Lou Rees swinging her hips behind him.

John Newman was a tall, bulky man. He looked down at Nora from a height. She had an impression of broad shoulders and greeny hazel eyes. Warm eyes with reassuring, bushy eyebrows. She covered her fluttering stomach by concentrating on taking the tall glass from him.

"Nursing? Do you like it?" His voice was unaccented, polite. But kind. Maybe? There was something though. He was older than Rich. Older than other men she knew. Was he sophisticated? Was that it or was he just being polite?

Nora feared she would crush the slim stem between her cold fingers. She clutched it , concentrating on the cold coming from the ice that layered the drink in sparkling slivers. Above the pinkish liquid, small chunks of delicate fruit floated. A twist of glazed orange looped the rim.

What about her Confirmation pledge? She had broken it with Babycham once and had shandies in the pub. But gin. Giggles were hastily choked back at her predicament.

"Taste it", John Newman urged. "It's delicious". His low voice was comforting. She trusted him.

She sipped carefully. He laughed; a deep, belly laugh. Heads turned.

"It was your face", he apologised but still smiled down at her.

No wonder. The cool drink sent rushes of pink pleasure down to her toenails, to the tips of each strand of hair, to each fraught vein in her body. The fragrance from the concoction of the fruit made her feel she was drifting with palm trees.

The room had filled up. Lou Rees was jiving with Rich Taylor, her round backside gyrating with passionate energy.

"Oh! You're from Ireland?" John Newman said. "Is that why you're wearing green?" His voice was teasing. She didn't bristle, as usual. He had not said "Island" like most Welsh and English people. He had the correct enunciation on the "r".

There was something about him; non-insular, unjudging, slightly aloof, alone. It was different, soothing. It was so tedious, tiring, always explaining, being angry, defensive.

"Are you going to San Francisco", the singer invited. They danced. She only came up to his breast pocket. He had been to Dublin once, he said, making small talk. He described a wide, sweeping river, bridges, quays beside the docks, places she did not know.

"And there was this bookshop." His voice was preoccupied even though he continued to look down at her. "There were books on stalls outside as well as inside. As if they'd spilled over. It was full, full of books".

There was a different tone in his voice. She could feel herself relaxing. Never had she met a man who talked about books, except Megan Owens's father. But not in this way. Tender?

"It was there I first bought 'On the Beach'."

"Nevil Shute? You like Nevil Shute?"

"Do you?"

She nodded, glowing. He was startled. "Really?"

"Oh, yes."

She had read "On the Beach" first. They stared. The coincidence.

Virginia McKenna was just as she imagined in "A Town Like Alice". He wasn't sure. They sparred. She let him off with a few points because he wanted to talk it out at length.

With two more drinks they idled over to a corner near a porthole. He was talking, talking. She was nodding, filling in names of Russians, places in America, grand Victorian houses.

He knew more about Conrad. He knew Dickens in vast, panoramic detail.

The room had darkened. Couples were snogging. The big-wigs had departed. So had Lou Rees and Rich Taylor. Nora didn't care. The light illuminating the ship filled the porthole, sometimes illuminating him, sometimes her.

She had pulled her hair out of the narrow French pleat and it fell around her face, guarding her. Her jacket was gone. She was glad she had taken Cas Jones's pretty blouse with the stand-up pleated collar.

His face had lost its serious, studiously grown-up look. It became expressive as he said how he could imagine being ensnared – he used the word selectively, deliberately – by Emma Bovary. But Sonya in "War and Peace"...there was something...

She confided that Pierre was absolutely her favourite man.
"Absolutely?"
She laughed. They danced. Slowly now, her head on his chest.
Her hair was like autumn, he said, touching it softly. They stopped.
His mouth came down and down. Slowly. She had to stand on tip-
toe. His lips were gentle. They touched hers, brushed the length of
her mouth. A caress it was. No tongue pushing at her or hard teeth
grinding into hers. It was silk and cool. Playing lips; like violins.

Her hand seemed small grasped in his large capable one. They
went along narrow corridors, the sea on one side, passing fumbling, giggling couples. In his cabin she gasped at the racks of
books, all carefully cordoned in with narrow frames.

"The weather", he said. "It can be bloody rough." He touched
them and patted them. He showed her his book bag in the corner
of the tiny room. He had borrowed Somerset Maugham's idea, he
said. It had most of his favourites. He was always adding new ones
and subtracting with great difficulty.

Even when he took off his heavy jacket, she was not afraid. They
sat back on the narrow bed. Her head lay on his chest, under his
chin. An arm held her closely and easily. His fingers traced her
eyebrows, nose and cheekbones.

They talked, sipping pink gin from one glass. He picked out a bit
of green fruit and put it between her lips. She felt like Eve.

They talked slowly, meandering through bits of their lives. He
had only been an officer for two years. Not like Rich or the rest. He
came from a two-up, two-down in Stockport. One sister married.
His mother worked hard; in a post office by day and dress-making
by night. His father was...feeble.

At 16 he joined the Merchant Navy. Correspondence courses
and blistering hard work. Sometimes a shroud came down on his
voice.

She looked at his hands, smooth now but broad and large. His
nails were perfect; long and tailored. They touched while continuing to talk.

She told him her secret ambitions, other secrets, bits of childhood. She told him about Alun, her medical student, his obsession
with the Welsh language, his shyness. How they were vague com-
panions with nothing but hospital gossip and people to unite them

except about once a month when he would get all worked up and be endlessly sorry afterwards.

With his firm lips he stroked her forehead. For fun, he counted her eyelashes. Every one. Five hundred and sixty-seven? She laughed up at him and then was silent with wonder. She felt his Robert Mitchum nose, shaped and reshaped his bushy eyebrows.

"They're like ditches", she whispered. "Those small ones at the side of the road. Nice, nice ditches." They were perfectly blended into a question mark.

SUDDENLY, from far, far away, from the kaleidoscope they were travelling in, she pulled away in panic. The stark lights outside the ship had gone out and the cabin was lightening with the grey dawn. God. She'd be missed. She could see Matron's implacable face. She would be sacked. What would she tell them at home.

He stayed as he was; casual, unmoving. "It's no good. The door is locked. I'm taking you to Lisbon. And then to Casablanca". He relented, chuckling at her. Standing up, his head touched the ceiling. He put his hands on her shoulders.

"It's only half-past five. I'll get a taxi. It will be all right."

She calmed.

The taxi swirled swiftly through streets now graced with romance behind their tired doors and wrinkled curtains. They sat apart on the back seat, fingers entwined. The taxi driver did not intrude on their silence. Again and again, they looked at each other; sometimes serious and searching, sometimes smiling. Their fingers knotted, then relaxed. He stroked her palm with his thumb. She shivered.

The taxi waited outside the gate and he walked quietly up the fire escape with her. It was not unknown for Night Sister to make an early morning round and close the door if she found it open. It swung in at his touch.

Without a word they sat on the top step, looking out over the city. Lights were going out. Ambulances were screaming in.

"I would love Lisbon."

He nodded slowly. "I know".

He put his hands around her face. "I know. You know I would too."

She nodded.

She watched him all the way down. He paused at every turn and looked up. When he was gone and she heard the taxi start she went inside. The mirror showed a different Nora. Dishevelled and dreamy; the watchful, careful look gone.

At breakfast Lou Rees was defiant, defensive. "I had to leave, didn't I. Couldn't find her." The others stared. Nora smiled. They were perplexed and then turned away to hear every last detail of Rich Taylor.

Nine days later there was a letter in her pigeon-hole in a grey envelope with neat black writing." I am on my way to Lisbon", it started. She skipped it until the end. "Be happy. I wish I could wave a wand to keep you as you are. Go back to Ireland. Have lots of children. Read them stories. I can still hear your voice. I hope you won't forget me but that is selfish. God bless you."

The green acid flavour of the mint from the pink gin pierced her tongue. She ran upstairs and hid the letter deep under her mattress.

LUCKY SINGING

Noel McFarlane

Dear Jacob,

It appears that I've just returned from my Christmas sortie to Dublin, Ireland, but really, that's only a guess. I remain seriously disoriented. I seem to be in my apartment as I write, by the window where we've talked so often. A slow, immensely silent fall of snow has just begun to fill the night here now, smothering the lights of the Jersey Shore, falling lazily through the streetlight amber, falling endlessly into the black Hudson.

My mind is spent utterly, everything has an ethereal aura. I look like a bum.

I do not have memories of those three days, I re-experience a series of bizarre tableaux. I perceive them chiefly through a haze of unprofessional, exasperated puzzlement, and a new, autumnal, "artistic" melancholy. I still smell alcohol. They clubbed me to my knees with drink.

Jacob, I could not really figure one of the bastards out, they would not stop spinning, they would not stop singing. Geraldine says: Why do you have to poke, fiddle and feck (trans: to touch interferingly) at everything and everyone? Weren't they only enjoying themselves, sure wasn't it Christmas? But Jacob, it wasn't Christmas, it was them. Three hundred dollars an hour I command, from the most celebrated and committed neurotics in Manhattan, and I could not get a functional, meaningful handle on one of "her people". One moment of deduced certainty would have fulfilled me. Instead, they crippled me with beauty.

As I wrote you previously, I went to Dublin with Geraldine to "display" for her family, my prospective in-laws. I think you met her once in the early stages (hair like polished sequoia, good teeth, great soul, tenacious mind, paradisal torso), you would remember if you had. Relax, she told me, they only want a lookatcha. And remember, these aren't your crowd from the Village, the painters that won't paint, the dancers that won't dance, the birds that can sing and won't sing, just give yourself a bit of a break out of that and relax.

I was indeed intent on relaxing, for calm is a requisite of intuitive seeing, as you know. I was keenly interested in the family as crucible. Well, you would, wouldn't you? But wait, Jacob, what a selfish schlemiel I am, even though I am beset. How was Hanukkah in Saudi? Your mother calls me for reassurance after every news show on "the situation": whenever Henry Kissinger is on, I have to spot her fifteen milligrams of Valium. I do my best with her. I tell her you are quite safe out there, that the army doesn't put its expensively educated, newly graduated shrinks into battle zones. You know that she responds to pragmatism best – the brand of the camps, again. So I lie a little. It is for love.

Your last letter says you're working out of a tent. I can hardly imagine. My patients won't divulge their names unless they have their tushes in one of those thousand-dollar New Age pseudo-thrones from Ethan Allen, while surrounded by twenty-five thousand dollars worth of "permission-indicating" South American folk art.

Geraldine despises them, I'm afraid. It's a difficulty. And, of course, immediately upon meeting her, they pant and drool after her effortless certitude: I know, she says, they're gas (trans: humorous). She had a wonderful time in Dublin, of course. She's sleeping now. When I saw her sleeping earlier, I could not rid my mind of what her father (aka Guard Tumelty, the Super Tumelty, Mister Tumelty) bayed at me over the endless, raucous communal singing and the blaring TV. He is a detective. His eyes rove constantly, like searchlights; I saw at once that they are utterly unconnected to his thoughts. He is a brute of a man, rigorously mercurial. He said: So, I hear tell you want my young one's hand, wha? Well, you've had everything else, doctor, be all accounts.

And then, an unselfconscious display of dentures, a jailer's cackle.

I SLEPT through most of the flight (I had tap-danced for half-a-dozen of my very surliest suicidals all day). The passengers were clearly Irish, all right. I hazily recall great gales of mindless communal singing from various parts of the aircraft: "Jingle Bells" and "White Christmas" were popular, of course, as was a positively Bavarian concoction about "The One Road". But, from those who sounded drunkest, I'll stake my reputation on the fact that I heard Catholic hymns, bellowed, sourly, in Latin! A thought: how we love our jailers, for where would we be without them? Answer: terrified by freedom!

Serious turbulence brought me to semi-wakefulness at some point. I recall seeing an entire aisle of them, probably a family, all in desiccated Christmas party hats: they were staring wide-eyed at nothing, like snared animals, as they carefully rode the jolts. Empty bottles clinked at their feet, having overspilled their tables. I noted that while their left hands clutched glasses containing morbidly large doses of alcohol, their right hands fidgeted in the gloom under the seats – they were fingering their prayer beads!

However, my experience upon touching tarmac in Dublin was particularly unique. From the rumpled, suddenly grinning ranks came an explosion of intense applause! I was close to astonishment. Do they do that every time they touch down, I asked Geraldine. She supposed so. But what did it mean, I asked. Could it be that they were expressing gratitude to the pilot for, essentially, not killing them? She whitened her lips. If so, didn't this betray a very unusual group demeanour or picture of the group self, I mused. Give it a rest, Theo, Geraldine said. But surely they knew the pilot couldn't hear them, anyway, I said, it was like children applauding in the movie theatre. Now that's enough, Mr Cleverality, she hissed, and it the mouth (trans: threshold) of Christmas.

There appeared to be a thousand members of her extended family waiting in a wary silence in the airport: I felt like Michael Caine in "Zulu". I knew many from photographs. Geraldine is the third youngest, Jacob, in a family of nine, *nine!* the married members of which carry on the torch of unremitting reproduction. They had all been drinking.

As I neared the group and began the ceremonial handshakes, something unusual led me to peruse the faces twice. I suspected initially that they were congenitally wall-eyed, or maybe even drunker than they appeared, but then I began to accommodate the reality of the matter – they were staring, in helpless fascination, at my nose.

Even her father, standing there in Prussian, patriarchal hubris, re-lented momentarily in his compulsive professional scanning of the other passengers to fix speculatively on it. And how is the man? he asked enigmatically. Man, I thought, what man? So I hung clever and wished him happy holidays. What appeared to be a frisson of comprehension, or relief, immediately suffused the troupe.

Well, happy em holidays, they said, with pure Elizabethan vow-els, as they shook my hand and stared at my hooter, many adding strangely: and fair play to you, fair play to you now.

Geraldine was obliviously aglow. As she approached her father, the giant looked warily left and right, allowed a momentary emo-tional liquefaction, muttered something about a chicken (strange!) and engulfed her. I immediately sought signals of sib jealousy among the others, but noted none, just an unusual stoic acceptance of the primary place I had always suspected her of occupying with "Me Da".

OUTSIDE, the peculiarly wet, piercing chill was a shock, but the atmosphere amid the airport throng, of Christmas bustle and warm expectation, almost dissipated it. The family poured itself into a series of illegally parked cars, and, to my surprise, a large blue official police truck driven by a furtive man in a rumpled uni-form, who confused me deeply by exuding an aura of unrestrained criminality and stealth. How is the for-um, he demanded heartily, adding, and happy whatever you're havin' yourself.

Downtown Dublin on Christmas Eve called to mind the Day of the Dead in Mexico City, but without any apparent religious inhi-bitions. The young were everywhere. Inebriated battalions of them marched about aggressively, bawling songs. Reeling figures palmed off walls, like injured running backs trying to slip tackles. There was candid drinking on the sidewalks, urination, passionate embracing, vomiting, and this inevitable, unending, frenzied sing-ing. Aw, she's hoppin' all right, said the uniformed man very rap-idly (opaque, Scandinavian-style accent, I thought, and he seemed to flaunt it). I hear tell tis dog wild in the Shtates, he said. I agree, I said cleverly.

My description of the dwellings in their home neighbourhood (Wightwall or Whyhall or somesuch) as townhouses, sparked volcanic hilarity among the driver, Geraldine's punkish cousins and others whom I did not know in the wired-off back of what they called "the wagon". We drove through chilly, pungent smog in what seemed like a labyrinth in a labyrinth. We stopped outside a house, where Geraldine's father stood in wait like a murderous sentry. I noticed as I hurried indoors from what was clearly serious air pollution that the house did not have a Christmas tree in its front window, as did every other house on the block.

The scene inside was to become a commonplace over the next two days. It engulfed and drowned me.

A compact strata of children and infants writhed on the floor of "the kitchen" like snakes in a pit. A vast, perplexing kaleidoscope of people drinking morbidly spoke *at* each other without listening (this, especially, Jacob, struck mortally at my personal and professional heart) alternating swiftly between what was termed "the slaggin" and remarkable familial tenderness and insight: and there was individual and choral singing, some of it sublime and transporting (I recall, through the sparkling gaiety of early drunkenness, the shady uniformed policeman suddenly throwing wide his arms and exploding into Puccini a foot from my face) and some of it was infantile, drunken drech.

And of The One Song that Redeemed All But Me, more anon.

As soon as I entered the house I noted the curious absence of any sort of Christmas decoration. Also, there were ghostly rectangles on the papered walls, where, I was sure, pictures had recently hung. The Super Tumelty, holding an unmarked bottle of clear liquid and glasses (they looked like doll's house props in his paws) quickly cornered me, a drop now in hearty welcome, he said, and poured a huge measure. Geraldine had warned me precisely, twice: Now don't refuse a drink or two – they'll think you're either an oul' oddity or an alcoholic.

I drank as he did, quickly: it approximated to drinking fire. The second shot tasted, I felt, of trees, then bluish, pristine air. So, how is tricks anywah, he said cagily. Tricks? I said. The line of work, he said. Oh, I said, fine, and you? He shook his great head. Aw, sure our hands is tied, he said, our hands is tied at every turn. He lumbered off, the bottle raised before him like a prow.

I said to Geraldine: do you guys not put up Christmas stuff in this house? It's gas, she said, they don't want to, like, upset you. Upset me? I said. Well, she said, me Ma told me she found out "your people" don't believe in Christmas, she even took down her Sacred Heart! I was staggered. She sniggered.

I began to note a certain scintillation in the air, as though mood, the sadness of the evanescence of the moment, could sparkle in the very oxygen. Distance, then intellection, began to fluctuate curiously. I recall then the Super Tumelty slicing professionally through the throng towards me with the bottle raised; I recall laughing recklessly; I recall kicking accidentally against a carton pushed under the tub in the bathroom and finding the pictures there (Christ and his heart, Christ and his mother, Christ with his bleeding palms). I then recall the sudden silence as I handed them with formal care to Mrs Tumelty in the kitchen: Go ahead and hang these up, I had said (according to Geraldine), let each believe in anything, for I believe in everyone. Anyway, it's his birthday, isn't it? A storm of laughter, backslaps, I was a terrible man, an awful man, a great man for "a nerve doctor", they wouldn't be up to me, givis a song, have another and then a flood of childhood regression, the encompassing smell of my father, the smell of safety, as I was carried bodily by the Super Tumelty to a dark room filled with other sleepers – no, they were coats.

I WOKE with no hangover, but with a feeling of lightness, of intellectual potency. Then, as I "remembered", I uncovered a large scab of guilt. I went forthwith to the kitchen to confront this guilt. Picking through the carpet of children, I was shocked to find (1) that it was midday and (2) that many "visitors" seemed to be still there (or perhaps they had left and returned) along with what Mrs Tumelty termed "the second shift". I expressed sorrow for my behaviour generally and was immediately awash in forgiveness (how else would anyone survive there?): Twas jit lag, twas jit lag, gushed the singing policeman, who now wore an utterly disreputable suit.

The family, I was confounded to learn, had already toured several graveyards that morning for a cheerful seasonal visit with their multitudinous dead. So, the Shinto angle! I resolved there and then to attempt to desist from any further professional evaluation. Compared to these people, Jacob, the Jews are an open book.

There was a Christmas tree in the "parlour", smelling like Maine and as bright as Broadway. There were ridiculous Santas on the walls, Christ with his heart, Christ with palms displayed (Oi, I should be so lucky!) and drunken paper streamers on the ceilings. The Super Tumelty cornered me once more, holding a teacup. I made this tay with holy water, he said foxily. He cleared his throat (I felt the vibration). Don't mind me asking you, he said, but are you allowed turkey? Isn't it the pig ye're not allowed?

Acceptance defeats perplexity, I was learning, Jacob, and merely said yes.

A NOTABLE trio entered as I finished my second cup of "tay". Two were clearly detectives. They wore enormous, shapeless jackets and a sense of stoicism that I liked intuitively, or perhaps it was the tay about its work: the third man, a tired, shabby young man in denims, wore handcuffs.

The Super Tumelty, who had been reading a newspaper in a show of furious suspicion, greeted them heartily. He then offered the young man his chair! Well well! He left the room as the handcuffs were removed. Through the crowd, which was, I noted painfully, beginning to talk *at* each other again, I saw a child offer the trio cake from a plate. The disreputable policeman made his way surreptitiously across the room, shook hands with the young man, spoke to him briefly and then slyly folded money into the young man's breast pocket.

I had thought initially that the young man was unwashed, or badly birthmarked (they live with anything that doesn't kill them immediately) but as I headed for the bathroom I recognized the unmistakable stain of Kaposi's sarcoma on his jaded face, his neck, the back of his hand. His breathing seemed sadly laboured.

There and then, Jacob, there was an agreeable rediscovery of self and mission: I am proud to say that he looked just like my kinda guy; his eyes were my workshop, he could make his pain mine if he so wished.

The Super Tumelty re-entered, and with a self-conscious, botched attempt at a flourish, presented him with a crystal goblet and quickly filled it. I introduced myself as I passed, I was Theo Schrine, shrink and medical doctor, if there was anything I could do, he could ask. Well now fair play to you, he said. And then, to one of his "escorts": Is this the Harry that doesn't agree with Christmas? The policeman, quickly: Now Lucky, whist like a good man.

I STOOD in acute puzzlement at the bottom of the stairs by the front door, examining a plastic object which was screwed to the wall and which seemed for all the world to be a small fingerbowl. A fingerbowl on the wall? Well, even they wouldn't put a bird feeder indoors, I decided. A voice spoke suddenly at my ear. The stealthy policeman in the disreputable suit had materialized soundlessly there. Ya bless yourself wihha, he said, tis for holy water, I'd dimonstrate only I've a whole lohha drink took and I wouldn't have an hour's luck. He undid the bottom buttons of his steamboat gambler's "waistcoat". He said: No doubt you know the young lad inside has the AIDS? I did, I said. Ah, he's game ball, he said, and I'll tell you why. He has a young lad of five years. Says he to me once, I'm happy enough, Bat – I've someone to folly me other than the Drug Shquad! We feel for him.

THE ONE Song That Redeemed All but Me was called for in defence of peace, as darkness gathered. The Super Tumelty had broken up a scuffle using only a magic mantra: Ah lads, lads, the holy season! While he had the gathering's attention, he placed a paw on his massive chest elegantly, as though about to sing. Instead, he boomed: And now, a parting song before the bit of dinner. I call on Mr Lucky Burke to fill the bill. Good order please. There was an immediate tumult of urging, Man Lucky! More power Lucky! Sing out Lucky! Yes, Lucky!

Lucky, I thought, indeed.

The young man seemed very drunk now, or weary. He placed his crystal goblet on the floor and his hands on his knees. He reclined his head slightly and began to stare directly ahead, with extreme avidness. I suspected he was seeing things. He was, Jacob – I know that now. He was communing with whatever transcending thing, with whatever wordless, vital cognizance that had banished his anger and filled him with a sweet acceptance.

For Jacob, I heard this sweetness overflow into the waiting silence. He began to fill the room with a brown river of sound. It awed me. The intensity, the compass, was so new to me. The song flowed with the slowness innate to deep things.

> *On Raglan Road, of an autumn day,*
> *I saw her first and knew*
> *That her dark hair would weave a snare*
> *that I might one day rue.*
> *I saw the danger and I passed*
> *along the enchanted way,*
> *And I said let grief be a fallen leaf,*
> *at the dawning of the day.*

I WAS mesmerized, smitten, then devastated – and this, Jacob, is what abides. I could not but watch the Irish as he sang: some closed their eyes, smiling with the pleasure of the pain of it, weeping, drinking deeply, smelling their children's hair.

I did not know and do not know now, Jacob, if this is in some way "of" them particularly, this faculty to bear witness to elemental sadness, this capacity to shape enigmatic acceptance into what shines and is exquisite.

Geraldine was watching me. I knew she would be. She knew that I knew that she knew my precise anguish and yearning as I listened to dying Lucky singing: what he poured out so sweetly into adoring silence, I was condemned to poke, fiddle and feck for, amid self-doubt, resistance and insult. She came and kissed me. It was almost enough.

Thus, old friend, the snow falls for me tonight like the shattered atoms of something I had placed high above and worshipped.

I may have to go and live with them, you know, and learn to sing.

Love,

Theo

THIRTY-SIX BY THIRTY-SIX

Arthur Reynolds

FOUR men and their dogs and a laden ass paid no attention to the soaring gulls above as they went down the path to Dunquin quay on Kerry's Dingle peninsula. Four nods they gave me as they passed, but I followed when they had rounded a bend.

On the little quay they put down their belongings and slowly unloaded the ass. I noticed mattresses, barbed wire, a fishing net, a sack of flour, a bag of food, a few pairs of sheep shears and a tattered copy of Old Moore's Almanac.

I was in the area to record how a sail was rigged on the Kerry currach. At that time, outboard engines were beginning to spread, and I thought that the currach sail would disappear altogether.

The currach had an important role to play in small coastal communities which possessed no harbour, or only poor shelter from the wrath of the waves. Many races have devised their own portable boats for this reason – although not all are descendants of Euphrates craft, which is believed to be true of the coracle and currach.

Jack Tyrrell, the distinguished naval architect from Arklow, once assessed the currach's design for me. It was, he said, the very best craft which the Kerry fishermen could build with the tools and materials available to them. "If you open a flour bag down the sides", he explained as we sailed up the Irish Sea, "it will fit round the frames of a currach and join to both gunwales. All you need then is a needle, thread and tar."

As I watched the dark-clothed group of men, with their dogs and their ass, I thought of the wicker craft of ancient Iraq. Nothing passed between us until I spoke to the eldest, a man of about seventy.

"Have you no Irish?" he replied. "Is there no Irish left in Dublin?" Then he answered my question. He pulled the peak of his cap down, and glanced over to the Blasket islands.

"We're going back in to our house on Inishvickillaun to shear, but we live most of the year on the mainland now. The government moved us some years ago."

He went to join the others, who were waiting beside one of their half-a-dozen currachs which rested, upturned, on wooden supports. The three young men crawled under a boat, and each put his shoulder to a seat.

"Anois", said one, and six legs straightened under the whale-like hull and marched in short rhythmic steps along the quay to the slipway. A handful of water was splashed on the bow before the boat was launched.

I helped to fend off the boat from the concrete quay while the gear was loaded and the dogs were tied under the seats. "How will you spend the time after the day's work?" I asked.

Taking his pipe from his mouth, the old man looked at the youth seated in the bow. "Padeen is a fine singer. Mick there tells great stories. He has the poetry too."

The man stepped into the honoured seat in the stern, and the boat bobbed on the swell for a few moments before the oars and the tide drew it towards the islands.

My mind went back to childhood adventures inspired by reading Muiris O Suilleabhain's "Twenty Years A-Growing". There was the account of the lads in a boat trying to appease an over-friendly whale. Throwing in their dog might work, they thought. The richness and contentment of island life, as described also by Peig Sayers and Tomas O Criomthain, made it my Utopia. I was too young and innocent then to know it could not last.

As I stood on the quay watching the oars rising and falling in unison, the contrasts in this and another lifestyle grew wider as the boat got further away. Indeed, little did I know that the gap was to be accentuated perhaps even more markedly a short while later.

It was as much out of curiosity as anything else that I followed the ass as it set off slowly but purposefully up the cliff path and along the road. When it reached Kruger Kavanagh's pub my own gait flagged and I stepped into the cool darkness. While himself pulled my drink, I went over to examine a small portrait of oils of Kruger hanging on the wall.

"An artist from the BBC painted it", he said. "Came here on holiday and had me sitting still for an hour on five mornings while he worked."

The face that revealed much of a colourful life changed to match the expression on the fine portrait – not that I had any doubt whatsoever that it could be anybody else but the Kruger Kavanagh.

His was not a face that an amateur painter was likely to meet casually in stately Portland Place, where the BBC had its dignified London studios.

Kruger's likeness was unlike anybody's. I thought that if Da Vinci had seen it, he might never have spent four years working on Mona Lisa.

A glass touching the table attracted my attention to a stetson-hatted man of about 65 years sitting in a corner with a thumb stuck in his braces.

"Do I hear you saying, sir, that that portrait there took five mornings?"

"That it did", said the Kruger with a twist of the chin. "Five mornings."

"Do you know", came the drawl from the semi-darkness, "in the States you can get a scenery picture – thirty-six by thirty-six – painted in one morning?" He was holding his hands about a yard apart as he spoke.

"Thirty-six by thirty-six", he repeated.

LEONIE

Declan Burke-Kennedy

THE first real obstacle was Leonie's door. A strip of light beneath it told me she was still awake: probably examining her teeth in a hand mirror or lying in a slip reading some of the love comics I'd seen on her dressing table one night.

That was the first night, when I'd woken up wandering about the strange house calling my sister, Angie. Leonie had leapt from nowhere at me as I appeared in her room and administered one of her stinging slaps on the face. "That's for spying," she had screeched, immediately lowering her voice: "I'll tell your Aunt Maeve you were creeping about the place, spying. The Captain will have something to say too, when he finds there's a spy in the house."

After she had steered me back to my room, she tucked me in and her tone softened. "You were just walking in your sleep, weren't you?" I was shaking too much to answer. "Poor mite. I'm sorry I flew at you, but you gave me a woeful fright. Always remember, in this house no-one's allowed leave their room after curfew. That's one of the Captain's rules, not just your Aunt Maeve's." Then she patted my cheeks with her strong warm hands and smiled before turning out the light.

Tonight there was no sound from her room. I waited to hear breathing or pages turning: nothing. Maybe she was downstairs and would catch me on the way out. The bare wooden floor chilled my feet. I'd have to risk it.

Holding my shoes in front on me, I tiptoed past her room and down the narrow staircase. The door that separated the rest of the house from what Aunt Maeve called the servants' quarters was

closed but not locked. The carpeted floors at this level made fur-
tiveness easier.

I stood outside Aunt Maeve's room and waited till I heard her
mumbling to herself. She always muttered in her sleep, even when
she dozed off after lunch in a deckchair on the verandah. I was
used to waiting for this signal before sneaking off to the stable or
the railway bridge. I usually timed my excursions well and was
safely back with a book on my lap before the crescendo that
marked the end of her slumbers: she would mumble great streams
of gibberish, louder and louder, until she woke herself with a sudden fright.

If I missed these stormy rousings and could not explain my absence, I faced being referred to the Captain when he returned from
Africa. He was in the Congo with the United Nations, teaching the
natives a thing or two. He would soon put an end to my unruly
behaviour, Aunt Maeve would declare and I wondered what tortures he employed to enforce order at home and abroad.

I stopped outside the Captain's dressingroom, just in case he had
come back unexpectedly since I'd gone to bed. In all the weeks
since I'd arrived I'd only ventured in there once, while Aunt Maeve
was in a muttering torpor one afternoon. It was strange to find the
room so spotless, with all its military books and maps in perfect
array. One side of the wardrobe was chock-full of uniforms of different colours and dimensions, as if my uncle could take on various
shapes and sizes when he was charging into battle; in the other side
I had found red-and-black hunting jackets, jodhpurs and enormous riding boots with wooden boot trees in the shape of human
legs. As I stood shivering outside this sanctuary the masculine
smell of leather polish brushed my nostrils.

I didn't dare put my shoes on till I reached the ground floor.
Then I tiptoed through the kitchen and stood on a chair in the pan-
try to reach the sugar lumps. My hands were shaking as I groped
about the shelves. Remembering that the mare liked sugar lumps
as well as carrots, I filled my pockets, taking care, as best I could in
the darkness, not to leave any tell-tale traces.

I reached out to unbolt the kitchen door, but the bolt was already
back. I made my way out, wondering what punishment Leonie
would face if Aunt Maeve knew she'd gone to bed and left the door

unlocked. I had heard her being scolded once for not wearing her maid's uniform right; another time my aunt had threatened to send her home for pilfering food for the gardener – and she gave in only when Leonie burst into tears, saying her father used to beat her when he had drink taken. Her lovely round eyes were red with tears and her cheeks flushed and moist for the rest of that day.

There was a bright August moon and the night air was sharp. It was exciting, even dangerous, to be out of the house so late: this was a real adventure. I ran down the garden and into the orchard. Looking back, I could see the light from Leonie's dormer room; the house, which had been so often a prison to me that summer, now seemed to be winking, quietly applauding my truancy.

Suddenly there was a rumbling, then a deafening metallic crash. From the shadows of a nearby railway tunnel a goods train burst into my line of vision and down into the valley beyond the orchard wall. Carriage after carriage hammered against the joints in the tracks. It was making its way out from Kildare to the dark plain of the Curragh. I stood stiff with shock – till only a fading rhythmic echo remained. Even then my knees were still shaking; to steady them I sat down on the damp orchard grass and leaned against the trunk of a crab apple tree.

THE day I arrived I had stood on the platform with the Captain's note in my hand, as the train puffed and creaked its way out of Kildare station.

Estimated time of arrival, 1500 hours. You will be met by my aide, Corporal Dwyer. He will escort you first to the barracks; from there you will be accompanied home on foot by one of the domestic staff. If you are to continue living with us after the holiday, I will arrange for your winter clothes to be collected at a later date. That decision will be made on the basis of your conduct over the summer months under the guidance of your Aunt Maeve. My best wishes to your father and sister.
   Your caring uncle,
    Frank (Captain Francis D. Connolly).

CORPORAL Dwyer turned out to be a stocky man with a tanned face and a hoarse, smoker's voice. "So you're the visiting dignitary

I was dispatched to collect," he said, rolling a cigarette as he eyed me up and down. "I swear to God. Well, come on. Don't just stand there. I was told to bring you to the barracks to inspect the guard of honour. You better pull up those socks before you meet the Captain or you could be court-martialled. He's a real stickler, your uncle. A real stickler, so he is."

We drove to the military barracks in an army jeep, racing across the side roads of the Curragh at such speed that I held onto my seat. "See that there," Corporal Dwyer said, screeching the jeep to a halt and pointing to an enormous crater in the grass beside the road. "That's where a German pilot ditched a bomb after a mission up North during the War. That was near on twenty years ago, so it was. We heard the explosion in our billets and thought: 'Holy Mary and Joseph, Dev's changed his mind and declared war. The question is, who will we be fightin', the Germans or the Brits?' "

In the barracks that first day, while I was waiting for my uncle, I watched a company of recruits being trained for parade by a squat Drill Sergeant with a strong Scottish accent. Lighting up another cigarette behind my back, Corporal Dwyer whispered in my ear: "Paddy the Scotchman, we call him. He grew up in Glasgow and fought in the British army during the War, so he did. You'll hear some choice poetry in a minute or two, I swear to God." I was sitting on a bench at the edge of the square and, once or twice, while demonstrating a movement, the Sergeant caught my eye and winked when the men's backs were turned.

"Christ in Heaven," he bellowed at one stage; "d'ye call this a straight line? It's as crooked as a cow's piss in snow." When one of the recruits laughed, he charged up to the unfortunate soldier and roared commands in his face, ordering him to stand to attention, turn left, turn right, march in place and present arms over and over again, till I thought the man would collapse with exhaustion. Then he yelled similar orders at all the men and I noticed a coating of white saliva forming on his mouth and flying in all directions, often into their faces.

Eventually he slowed down his commands to a more human pace. "The important thing is to stand bolt upright, straight as a die," he insisted in his stern Scottish voice. "Imagine ye're tryin' to pull a six-inch nail out of a wall with the cheeks of yer arse." The whole line broke up in laughter and this time the Sergeant smiled too. He winked in my direction before dismissing the drill, much to the loud relief of the recruits.

My uncle appeared shortly afterwards and Corporal Dwyer, cupping his cigarette furtively in his hand, jumped to attention, clicked his heels and saluted. My uncle saluted less formally and sent the Corporal on an errand. He looked me over then, examining me from head to toe for a long while before declaring in an even louder voice than the Sergeant's: "Well, young man. What do you think of army life? No picnic, is it? This is the first step in turning namby-pambies into men." He was tall and broad-shouldered, with a blank face that reminded me of the cut-outs used by soldiers for target practice.

I shrugged and made a bleating response: "It's very ... nice, really." The back of my neck was suddenly moist.

He straightened my collar and patted me on the head, ordering me to take my suitcase and accompany him to the barracks gate. On the way he bellowed about how sad it was that my mother had died so young and how important it was that I didn't brood about it or become depressed. "We don't want you being a sissy. Tears are for girls, not for soldiers and men. You've a duty now to your mother's memory." I glanced about nervously to see if the whole barracks was listening.

My uncle continued: Aunt Maeve was my mother's sister and she would look after my education, depending of course on how well I behaved myself in Kildare over the summer; I was to do everything I was told and to show respect at all times; he was going to Africa with the United Nations, to put manners on the Congo rebels, and would be counting on me to acquit myself well; the alternative, of returning to Westmeath to live with my father, was not something that would be in my best interest — and he repeated that many times with minor variations: not *really* in my best interest; not *at all* in my best interest; *certainly* not in my best interest.

Corporal Dwyer was at the barracks gate talking to a young woman with curly black hair and bright round cheeks. She was carrying a navy raincoat over one arm and wore a white headscarf tied under her chin. The young woman backed away and the Corporal turned and saluted the Captain again. "This is Leonie," my uncle said. "She'll walk you to the house and show you to your room. It's a long walk, so leave your case and I'll bring it home later." He gestured to the Corporal, who picked up my suitcase and carried it away. My uncle turned and followed him, shouting back to me: "And remember boy, stand up straight. Don't slouch. We'll make a man of you in Kildare, you can be sure of that."

I was shy walking along the country roads with Leonie, especially when she pulled off her scarf and shook out her great crest of black curls. I was glad I was far away from my jeering schoolfriends in Westmeath. She had a pretty face and the kind of figure I'd heard older boys describing as "a real handful." She hummed a popular song over and over and swayed her hips to make her long skirt swirl around her legs. At one stage she picked some roadside flowers and even put one in the buttonhole of my coat. "Red matches your rosy cheeks," she said and laughed quietly to herself.

We said nothing for a long time and I thought she seemed impatient with the assignment of collecting me from the barracks. She vented her irritation by warning me of the consequences of breaking any of the Captain's rules. They were recited with a relish that I didn't understand, as I hadn't yet done anything to offend her.

"Why are there so many rules?" I asked. "It's not like that at home."

"Why, why, why," was all she chanted by way of a response.

"Did you spend much time with the Corporal?" she suddenly asked at one stage of the trek.

"Yeah. He's nice. He showed me where the Germans dropped a bomb."

"He brought you there?" she laughed; she seemed surprised. "Why do you think he's nice?"

"He's friendly. But he's not as funny as the Drill Sergeant. The Sergeant's a real character."

She seemed to lose interest then and I felt a great urge to tell her Paddy the Scotchman's secret of how to stand up straight, but I was not sure if that would be in breach of some rule or other, so I said nothing. Instead, I walked on in silence while she hummed "Daisy Dotes and Dosey Dotes" for the umpteenth time. I remember wondering if she even hummed it in her sleep. Or at Mass.

THE shock of the night goods train had passed but I was still shivering. Dampness from the orchard grass was seeping through my clothes. I thought of the stable and the warmth of the straw where the mare lay down to sleep. I'd better not dawdle: Corporal Dwyer had said she only lay down for an hour or so in the middle of the night. I got to my feet and checked my pockets: my supply of sugar lumps and carrots was intact. Then I ran out through the orchard gate and down the narrow laneway that led to my uncle's stables.

As I turned into the yard, a black cat leapt from a roof towards a sack of oats waiting to be stored. There was a great commotion and squealing in the darkness and then something scurried near my feet. I reached out and hoisted myself onto a ladder, just as an enormous rat whipped past me, the cat in hot pursuit. The pair circled the yard once and disappeared into the laneway. I marvelled at my good fortune in having found the ladder leaning against the door into the loft. Corporal Dwyer, who worked in his spare time as groom and general handyman to the Captain, usually put it away each evening before cycling back to the barracks – or, if he was on leave, to his mother's house in the town.

I found the mare lying down, just the way the Corporal had said she would be, and as the moonlight streamed into the stable, she looked in my direction and blinked her enormous eyes. If she stayed lying down in your presence, the Corporal had told me, it was a sign she liked you and trusted you. "Sarah," I whispered; "it's only me. I've brought you a midnight feast." The mare continued her long slow blinking but did not rise to her feet.

By way of a starter I offered her a carrot. She sniffed it briefly before twisting her huge upper lip around it and folding it into her mouth. I knelt on the straw beside her and laid my hand between her erect, flickering ears. She munched slowly and I was so happy that I laughed quietly to myself. The mare half-closed her eyes with pleasure and I felt fully accepted. "The sugar's for dessert. You can't have any till you eat your carrots," I explained, reminding her of one of Aunt Maeve's house rules. The horse munched on intently, as if to say: "You don't have to tell me the rules. I've been living here longer than you."

I don't know how long I stayed there then, stroking her enormous face and telling her how beautiful she was. Occasionally she expelled great gusts of air from her nostrils and, in case this might be a response in horse language to my declarations of love, I took deep breaths and exhaled in the same way. Eventually she laid her head down on the straw and I rested mine on her warm neck and closed my eyes.

I was woken by a scratching sound from the loft above the stable. Rats. They'd hardly come near me if I was lying beside so enormous an animal. The scratching continued. If they're rats, I thought, they must be in mortal combat. There was a gasping sound that seemed almost human. Then I heard a crescendo of shuffling and floorboards creaking.

The sounds disturbed the mare: she raised her neck from the ground and struggled to her feet. I stood beside her, clutching her mane. It was dawn and a cold light was inching through the stable door. I kept my eyes fixed on the manger, fearing that one of the rats might fall or be knocked down through the open trapdoor above it. The horse whinnied nervously and the commotion stopped. "Good girl, Sarah," I whispered. "You've frightened them away."

As I had often done to pull hay down for the mare, I climbed onto the metal bars of the manger and raised my head through the trapdoor. The loft was darker than the stable and I couldn't see much.

"What's that?" I heard a woman's voice ask from behind a mountain of hay. "Did you hear something?"

"Keep your hair on. It's only the fuckin' mare," a man's voice replied.

There was laughter then and a lot of rustling. I was sure now I recognised the voices.

"Holy Mary and Joseph, I swear to God. Lie straight, will ye girl. Pretend ye're tryin' to pull a six-inch nail out of a wall with the cheeks of yer arse."

The Corporal's words and his attempt at a Glasgow accent provoked such delight and laughter in Leonie that I wished I'd had the courage to tell her that joke the day she had collected me from the barracks. I stayed as still as I could, perched on the manger, till my eyes became more used to the darkness.

Later I slid quietly from my perch and tiptoed past the mare on my way back to the stillness of Aunt Maeve's house.

IT was a drizzly evening and Aunt Maeve and her bridge circle were on their third or fourth sherry.

"Well, what were we to do? We couldn't just build a moat about ourselves, however much we might have wanted to. We couldn't leave the boy at the mercy of a man like that. I said to Frank: what do you think? What do I think about what, he said. About Sally, I said. She was my sister after all, remember that. But she's dead, he said. I know that Frank, I said, I know. It's the boy I'm thinking about. The girl's old enough. And she's at boarding school. Well, you know what Frank's like. You might as well be talking to the barracks wall. If it's our duty, he says, we've no choice in the matter. We can't just build a moat about ourselves. I'll leave you to work out the logistics. It's your bid, Florry; I dealt didn't I? I'll leave you to work out the logistics. That's what he said."

Her friends nodded sympathetically, staring at the cards they were rearranging in their hands.

"I still say it's a saintly thing to do," one lady with a Northern accent said. "I'll bid one diamond." She held up her glass for a refill from the decanter which Leonie was carrying around the card table. "It can't be easy at your stage of life, Maeve. I mean settled as you are in your ways. You know what I mean. No, I'll go for hearts. Two hearts. It can't be easy at all."

The conversation seemed to follow Leonie and the decanter.

"It's enough to have lost a sister so young, Lord have mercy on her soul. And what a life she had, the poor creature, married to a brute the likes of that. Two hearts, did you say? I'll pass. Thank you, dear. What did you say your name was?"

"Leonie, Ma'am."

"A pretty name and pretty face."

"Thank you, Ma'am."

"But look on the bright side, Maeve. He's not a bad little lad. And maybe he won't turn out like his father. Two no trumps. Thank you, Leonie."

"Rule him with an iron fist, Frank says. Make sure you know where he is, every minute of the day. Leave nothing to chance. You never know what's in the blood. What was the last bid, two no trumps was it? Leave nothing to chance, Frank says. It's all in the pedigree."

Leonie set down the decanter and left the drawingroom. I slid from my hiding place behind the curtains, out the French window and across the lawn towards the orchard. There was still a steady drizzle but I didn't care.

Under the crab apple tree where I did most of my thinking, I wondered why the adventure had gone out of my life. In the last few weeks I'd stopped going to the railway bridge to watch the goods trains shunting up and down the sidings; I didn't want to spend time helping the Corporal in the stables and listening to his stories any more; and, even though my nocturnal excursion had never been discovered, I had no heart to revisit the mare.

I saw Leonie coming from the kitchen with a laundry basket and making her way to the end of the vegetable garden where the clothes-line hung, weighed down with fluttering sheets and towels. She was humming as usual and skipped as she walked, oblivious of the light rain. She stripped the line before turning towards Seamus, the gardener who came every Wednesday and Saturday evening and spent most of his time on his knees between rows of cauliflowers and cabbages. He was an old man with shrivelled hands who shuffled about in all weathers, mumbling and dribbling over his beloved plants.

Leonie stopped humming, set down the basket and crept up behind the stooped figure; when she was almost on top of him she said "Booh" and the old man looked up with a start and flashed a toothless smile at her. She reached back to the basket and from inside a tablecloth took some food wrapped in greaseproof paper and what looked like a sherry bottle. He snatched the offerings and stuffed them into the sack he used for weeds, glancing nervously in the direction of the house. He beckoned her close to him and whispered something in her ear that set the two of them laughing. Leonie skipped indoors and, even after the old man had resumed his cramped work, the garden was still echoing with her laughter.

I followed her into the kitchen and went to the sink to pour a glass of water.

"What do you want?" she asked in a gruff voice. She had taken off her white cap and apron and was pouting her lips in front of a small mirror above the Rayburn. She flounced out her curly hair and admired herself from various angles.

"Nothin'," I said. I drank the water without taking my eyes off her.

"What are you starin' at then?"

"A cat can look at a king. Or a queen for that matter."

She laughed. "You cheeky blaggard. So you're a cat, eh? Well, I'm sorry to tell you, Puss, that it's your bathtime. And Queeny's planning an early night, so you better not dawdle."

"When is the mare going to have foals?" I asked suddenly, for no reason that I could think of.

"The mare? I don't know. Was she ever brought to the stallion?"

"I don't think so."

"Well, in that case she won't be having any foals, will she?"

"Do mares always get foals if they go to the stallion?"

Leonie looked at me and laughed. "Not if they're careful."

I saw she liked this line of questioning, so I asked: "Why has Aunt Maeve no children?"

"How do I know? Maybe she was never brought to the stallion."

She laughed again and punched my arm playfully. "Come on, little quiz master. No more red herrings. Off you go to your bath."

On my way past the drawingroom door I noticed the voice levels were even higher than earlier. There seemed to be an argument going on, but it was impossible to pick up the threads: two of Aunt Maeve's bridge friends were talking at once. I went to the bathroom and turned on the two huge taps. The rush of brown-yellow water drowned out the voices below.

That night in bed I wondered if Leonie had gone to meet Corporal Dwyer. I couldn't help thinking of them climbing the ladder into the hayloft and taking off their clothes to lie in the hay together. They would startle the mare again and I wouldn't be there to console her. I remembered the softness and laughter in Leonie's voice, in contrast to her cold, impatient tone when she was talking to me — except for the night I'd wandered into her room and she'd come to tuck me in. I wished she was beside me now, leaning over me and talking gently.

I couldn't sleep, so I crossed the landing and knocked quietly on her door. As I expected, there was no reply. I turned the handle and switched on the light. I stood for a long time looking at Leonie's few personal belongings, her little jars of make-up, her dresses, her plastic jewellery. A metal alarm clock ticked loudly on the dressing table. I fingered some of the silky woman's clothes that were strewn about the room and flicked through the pages of her comics.

I lay on Leonie's bed then, reading a romance about a schoolgirl who was in love with a handsome riding instructor. The problem for the girl was that the instructor treated her like a child and didn't see that she loved him. I found this odd: the girl looked very old to me and had all the curves and shapes of a fully-grown woman. However, the story came to a happy climax one day, when the girl's horse bolted and the instructor had to chase after her and save her from being thrown. It was only when he saw her in danger that he realised he loved her: that was what he said to himself in the last frame of the story, which showed them as bride and groom on the steps of a church, smiling at all their friends.

Later that night I woke up in a sweat and from downstairs in the hall heard the sweetest voice I knew in the world making inquiries about me. I leapt from Leonie's bed and ran down flight after flight of stairs, tripping once or twice and shouting "Mammy, Mammy, Mammy!" Aunt Maeve was showing her friends to the door and they all stopped in the hallway and stared up at me in silence. I sat down on a step and pressed my head and shoulders against the wall to stop the shaking.

"Poor wee lad," the Northern lady said. "He's having a dream. You go to him, Maeve. We'll let ourselves out."

"I KNEW you were a spy, from the first day you came here," Leonie yelled at me early the next morning.

She was standing in my room and had pulled the bedclothes down to the bottom of the bed. Dawn light was piercing the curtains.

"What do you mean?"

"You told your aunt about me. You squealed on me to that silly bitch."

"I don't know what you're talking about."

I tried to snatch the blankets back over my legs but she reached down and threw them to the floor. It was only then that I noticed she'd been crying and her eyes were red. She was not wearing her white apron, nor the stiff white cuffs and cap that went with it.

"You told her I wasn't in my room last night and she sat up and caught me coming in."

I pulled myself up in the bed and said: "I didn't say anything about you, cross my heart."

Leonie lashed her great palm against my face. "That's for tellin' lies."

I suddenly thought of my father, staggering home in one of his drunken rages, towering over my mother and me. "I swear," I said, holding my cheek. "I could've told her. Maybe, I should've. Long ago. But I didn't."

Her hand was raised to hit me again, but she stopped. "Long ago? What do you mean long ago?"

"The time I saw you and the Corporal lyin' together in the hay-loft. You had no clothes on and you were breakin' the curfew. You nearly scared the livin' daylights out of the mare, only for I was there to keep her calm. I could've told on you then, but I didn't, I swear I didn't."

Leonie's mouth fell open and her round cheeks flushed a deep crimson. "What are you talkin' about, you little blaggard?"

My face was stinging now and I felt a bitter rage welling up in my chest. "You were carryin' on in the hayloft and I don't care if you get caught. I hope you get a baby and everyone knows you were at it." Leonie stared at me in silence. "If you don't believe me I can prove it. The Corporal told you the Sergeant's joke about pullin' a nail out of the wall. You needn't pretend you don't remember that?"

"Holy Jesus," Leonie said under her breath. "You're a spy alright, a master spy, worse than ever I thought. I was only talkin' about you prowlin' around my room last night, readin' my private diary and letters. That's all I thought you were up to."

"I never read your diary or letters," I said. "I don't even know where they're kept. I went into your room to read a comic and I fell asleep on your bed. I woke up later and came back in here."

"Well, you left the door open and the silly bitch saw I was out without leave — that's why she sat up for me. She must have come up here to see if you were alright. If you'd minded your own business and stayed out of my room, she'd be none the wiser."

She paced about the room, took a crumpled ten-pack of Sweet Afton from the pocket of her dress and lit a cigarette. For a while she seemed to forget I was there and looked like she was carrying on an argument in her head. With Aunt Maeve, I supposed. Or maybe the Corporal. Maybe they'd had a lovers' quarrel. Suddenly she stopped and noticed me watching her.

"I suppose you didn't do it deliberately. You were probably walkin' in your sleep again, is that it?" She stubbed out the half-smoked cigarette in the fireplace and returned it to the pack.

I lay back in the bed and Leonie pulled the clothes up around me. She sat in a chair staring at the wall and said nothing for a long time.

"I'm sorry I hit you," she said eventually and her voice was as soft as the night in the hayloft. "Are you goin' to tell on me? I suppose you will. I suppose it's all I deserve."

I shook my head. She looked at me with her big moist eyes and I thought of the mare blinking in the moonlight. If you bring her carrots and sugar, she'll let you lie down beside her, the Corporal had told me one day when we were cleaning out the stable together. Just like a woman, he said. They're all the same, he repeated over and over, spitting into the steaming manure pit. They have to be pampered or they won't let you near them. I swear to God.

"To tell you the truth," Leonie was saying. "I wouldn't be too sorry if the bitch fired me. I've an offer of work in Newbridge and I think I might take it up. It couldn't be worse than this madhouse. Or I might pack up entirely and go to Dublin. They've real jobs up there, with real pay. In factories and hotels. And I won't have to be a fuckin' skivvy for the rest of my life. I can live in a flat and come and go when I like."

"What about the Corporal? Will he go too?"

"How could he? He's married, isn't he?" She looked at me in silence for a moment.

"I thought he lived with his mother."

"The mother of his kids. He calls her Mother for some stupid reason. He's a real headcase, that man. I don't know why I got in with him in the first place. I must've been off of my head."

Leonie stood up from the chair and yawned. "Christ, I'm jaded. I can hardly keep my eyes open."

She flopped down heavily on the side of the bed, her back turned towards me. I noticed a hayseed in her hair and I reached up and took it out. Her hair was as soft and light as I'd imagined, not wiry like the mare's mane. She turned then, took my hand and kissed it. "Thanks," she whispered and I noticed tears welling up in her eyes. "You're not a bad sort, even if you're ..." She yawned again and I thought she was going to fall asleep.

"If you go, I'm leavin' too," I said quietly. "I'll go back home. I couldn't stand it here." I turned my face to the wall and for a few moments she stroked my hair. Then she kissed me on the back of the head and got to her feet again.

"I can hardly stand up straight," she said. "I don't know how I'll get through the day."

"I'll tell you what," I said, sitting up and doing the best Scottish accent I could manage. "Imagine ye're tryin' to pull a six-inch nail out of a wall with the cheeks of yer arse."

She laughed, clapped her hand over my mouth and suddenly grew stern again. "Mind your tongue, young man," she said. "Remember your Aunt Maeve's rule about barracks language. We don't want that kind of thing brought into this house, now do we? Well, do we?"

"No," I said, puzzled by the sudden change.

She stood grooming her hair in front of a mirror, combing it with her fingers for any further traces of her night's activities. When she was sure it was clear, she turned to me and said: "We'll bide by the rules and that way no-one will know of our secrets. You and your mare, me and my Corporal. You can visit me whenever you like and we'll read and tell stories to each other. We'll build a little moat around ourselves and when we're alone we'll do exactly as we please. That way we'll beat them at their own game, Aunt Maeve and the Captain, the whole fuckin' lot of them. No-one will suspect a thing. Is that a deal?"

I nodded uncertainly. I had made up my mind in the last week, sitting in the orchard under the crab apple tree: as soon as the Captain came back, I was going to go home and live with my father, whatever the consequences. The decision would be mine, not his or Aunt Maeve's. But my resolution wavered at that moment and, in ways that I could only vaguely sense at that stage, my life began to take a different course.

Leonie stopped in the doorway and smiled back at me; then she winked before closing the door gently behind her.

SATURDAYS

Mary Maher

IT was on Saturdays when the three of them were all together that the whole thing, the new family unit, began to gell: man and wife and child. By the time they were in their second autumn together, Saturdays had developed a rhythm, a snug and even humdrum ticking over that she loved and felt profoundly grateful for.

They started in a lazy way, rumpled with tea in bed and the radio and letting the baby chew over his bottle between them; then one washed up while the other dressed the baby for the trip to the shopping centre. It was amazing, and wonderful, how such an ordinary excursion had taken on such warm meaning.

They always did Quinnsworth first, taking their time about it, enjoying the whole debate on what was worth buying in bulk this weekend and what was ludicrously over-priced. The trolley filled up in a co-ordinated, comforting tumble, bright yellow labels testifying to the wisdom of generic brands. They had developed a tolerance for each other's ways that was full of charm for them; he had a truly childish habit of shoplifting, something small and edible usually, which she pretended to abhor. She insisted on expensive vinegar, cider or wine or tarragon.

They worked like a team at the check-out. She unloaded, playing every week the same game with herself: could she get all the fridge stuff in one lot, all the cleaning and toilet things in another, all the tins and packets together? She never could, quite, because he packed so swiftly and efficiently. The baby gnawed on his rusk and crowed, watching them.

When that was all bagged and tucked in the boot of the car, they toted the baby back inside and looked for the other bits and pieces, the ones that added to their aspirations and their life together. They got paté from the delicatessen and some special cheese, and maybe something wild, guava or marmalade chutney. They went to the good wine shop, then, and read all the labels and prices before selecting something really nice to supplement the two-litre supermarket plonk.

Then they had lunch, always, in the coffee shop; though it wasn't really lunch but more of a snack because the price of a slice of quiche, even, was crazy. Still, it was a weekly treat, and she almost always weakened and had something sticky while he teased her.

The coffee shop had been easier when the baby was smaller, when he lay there like a Christmas doll in his pram, and slept peacefully, and passers-by stopped to admire him. Now he clambered around and grabbed at things and they passed him back and forth and had to bounce him if he fretted. It was a relief when another, older child stopped at the table and the baby, arrested with the fascination of a new face, stilled himself and stared until they finished their coffee.

Then they strolled back to the car, dawdling because there was all the time in the world. Sometimes, not very often, she wanted to see what was in the boutique and occasionally she even tried something on. That was more to parade for him, she knew, than anything else. God knows she didn't require party gear or anything but jeans and jumpers these days. He was good-natured about it, though, and enjoyed it if the place wasn't too crowded, or the baby, as he said, driving him bananas.

More often they spent the time in the home-improvement centre. There invariably seemed to be something they'd overlooked last week, and in a way it was bewildering how much there was you'd love to buy if only you had the money. The cork tiles they had multiplied and subtracted now for every room in the house, but they still couldn't manage it, even for the bathroom.

The last stop was the newsagent's, where they bought a paper and she looked over the magazines but didn't buy any. They went home then, and really she preferred it when it was miserable and wet, the rain dribbling down the car windows, and he cursing gently at the wipers which never worked properly. A nice day, especially in summer, she told him, made you feel uneasy, as if you should be larking about at the seaside, but when winter was pulling around them, there were no such qualms because the best place to be headed for was home and a fire.

He laughed; he said affectionately she was a lazy bitch; you'd think to hear her there was something terrifying about doing anything healthy in the great outdoors. But it wasn't that, she knew, it was just that larking about seemed like something from a past life.

They had a short hassle of a time at home again, because unpacking was never so much fun as buying - you dreaded what you'd seen you'd spent, he said ruefully - and the baby was cranky and had to be put for a nap. They had to get the fire going and the chill off the room and she finished off a few bits of chores while he read the paper, snorting and rattling it when he didn't like what he read, reading bits aloud.

But it was still, in its ordinary way, the happiest of times. The day was of a piece, there was nothing that had to be done absolutely or rushed through. It was their own in a way nothing else was, because Monday to Friday was work and the time was laid out for you in patches, just like school; and on Sundays they always went up to her mother, which he hated but never told her. It was a gift from him to her, but she never knew about it; so as a gift, it was quite pointless.

Saturday was what they had, to watch themselves being a family. He pulled the curtains and shut the doors in the passages and spoke of insulation and other future prospects, and she did the fry, carefully and in order, putting all the crusty cooked things in the oven to keep warm before the eggs and tomatoes. They tickled and rocked the baby and bathed him and sometimes the genuine miracle of his existence would strike each of them, separately, just as it had the first week of his life. But usually he was just himself, part of them and they would watch with relief as the little mouth finally yielded its grip on the bottle and they could put him upstairs, "down for the night."

Then they opened the bottle of nice wine and had the late film and the fire to themselves; and themselves to themselves. It was the surest and safest and best of all possible worlds, and the weeping windy rain pounded away outside in wretched envy.

TARA STREET TAYLES

Seamus Martin

Drawings Martyn Turner

(After Geoffrey Chaucer's Canterbury Tales, verray looselie and baudilie)

Wherynne ye wryter lookes at ye lyves of travellours from ye Benne of Howthe to ye stronde at Braye.

This worke hath beene translated into ye Germayn tongue as Ein Fahrt an der Dart and into ye Moderne Englysshe of ye Citye of Dublynne as "A fawrt on the Dawrt".

Yt is dedicayted to ye people havinge ye exceeding straunge accent founde a longe ye Darte lyne in ye saide Citye.

Prologue

Aboard ye Darte which plyeth Northe and Southe,
Along ye Baye which formes ye Liffye's mouthe,
There crowdeth from ye earlie morninge lyte,
Until ye darkest,and ye blackest howre of nyte,
Ye hoardes of pilgrims who doth personly travaile,
And eache of themme to telle, doth have a tayle.

A bisy-nesse manne hath voyaged from ye Sowthe,
Unto his mansionne on ye Hille of Howthe,
He was no verray, parfit gentil knyght,
And as afar fromme house he wolde alyte,
His wyfe perforce aughte leve ye reddening coals,
And waite for him at station, with ye Rolls.

A Yuppie was there from Monkes Towne also,
That unto stockes and shayres had soon ygo,
His face in journall pynke wolde buryed be,
As he hunge to strappe with all alacritye,
But who wolde think, beneathe his pyn-stryped hose,
He lyked to weare ye wymmen's onder-close?

A verray awe-full Lecher rode ye traine,
With purpose for to gette himself a lain,
Resultante from his worke and from his pacience,
Lovers he hath at fyve and twenty stations,
And ye maydes as have ye Lecher well evaded,
Hath knowed him bye his mien...extreemely jayded.

A Philosphre hath journeyed downe ye lyne,
who bore ye Tewtonne nayme of Wittgenstein,
He prateth e'en unto ye childer smallest,
"Die Welt ist alles, was der Fall ist",
He studieth harde and with a grave intente,
Ye deepeste originnes of ye Dawrte accente.

Into ye towne each daye theyre goes a wyve,
Housbondes-at-church-dore she hadde lost fyve,
Well harde she strove ye Lecher to avoyde,
For with housbonde onlie wolde she be a joyed,
So daylie from Bath Avenue she wolde runne,
To a matrimoniale agente, her owne sonne.

Ye Bissy-nesse Manne

Tara Streete Tayles

Ye Bissy-nesse Manne's Tayle

My worke is harde, and full of enterpryse,
So unto ye tacks-man I do telle ye lyes,
I saye greate golde onne charytye I've spent
And paye mye tacks at less than tenne per cente
To house eache nyte, replete I *will* go
Well-dyned extensyvlie at Patrick Guilbaud.

And iffe at station's edge my wyfe is late,
Her tardinesse I soundlie wille berate,
And roare at herr with great and loude annoye,
As though shee were some one in mye employe,
And thenne to mansionne large I shalle repaire,
behaveinge lyke a greate and angrie beare.

But one certes nyte from Guilbaud's I lefte earlie,
Havinge paide a cruked Unione manne ryght dearlie,
Ye trayne at Howthe arrived to mete ye Rolls,
I left ye Darte with othyr, poorer soules,
And too mye greate dysguste there did I finde,
In backe seete, wyfe and Lecher all-entwyned.

Ryght sune, a chauffeure I was forssed to hyre,
And decke hym oute in gaudie, bryght attyre,
And what stucke moste of all, ryght in my throte,
I payde him for each tryppe, a tenne pounde note,
All this travaille did make me strongely feele,
That I sholde luke oute for a bettere deale.

True to Type

Ye Yuppie

Tara Streete Tayles

Ye Yuppie's Tayle

Whan I a stuidente was at Clongowe's Wude,
Ye maisters felt that I wolde do no gude,
This falsse and awe-fulle judgment they mayde there,
Havynge cawte me in my syster's brassiere,
My antient fathere, angried att their slyngs,
On my be-halffe, went out to pulle ye stryngs.

And thenne, despite my luve for lyngerie,
I was aprentyssed faste at S K C,
And sune in stockes and shares, I did ecksell,
Counfoundinge those who saide I'd not do well,
And as I journeyed up and downe ye lyne,
Ye bisy-nesse manne becayme my frend in tyme.

And att the vylest jounctuyre of hys lyfe,
When he hadde gayned a chauffeur, lost a wyfe,
At Buter's Towne ye trayn stopped suuddenlay,
My trowsers slypped, and shewed my negligée,
A curiouse glaunce was passed betwixte us bowthe,
And off togethyr boundedde we to Howthe.

Nowe far from the Eckschange's hotte imbroglio,
Fromme Eadair's Benne I menage hys portfolio,
He knowes not when I certifye hys countes,
I tayke my-selffe some passyng fayre amounts,
When he returns all bloted, fulle and sate,
He's onlie gladde ye Rolls is nevyr late.

True to Type

Ye Lecher

Ye Lecher's Tayle

For manie yeres I've sawte ye crowded traynes,
To brush up againste wymmen I'm at payns,
Of all the creature's Oure Goode Lorde protecks,
I surely am ye moste enslaved to secks,
For manne ytte ys an awe-full grieviouse penalty
To bee more randdier styll than John F.Kennedy

Alonge ye lyne my luvers are a plenty,
Amours I've had at stations fyve and twentie,
Att Killestere halte a servaunt mayde called Sadie,
Att Sandie Cove a buck-some wealthie ladie,
I squired a matronne fayre of Harmonne's Towne,
Wythe systers twynne in Dalkie bedded downe.

Wythe a Belfaste lass I have cavorted bonnilie,
That I espyed alyte ye trayn at Connolly,
And whenne ye Darte was barren I, fore-soothe,
Did rampage on ye West Lyne to Maynoothe,
On tryppes abroade I verraylie did fain,
to be ye knyght a pricking on ye plane.

But came ye daye whenn alle ye wymmen's dazzle,
Ytte truely hadde me beaten to a phrazzle,
And sune to settaille downe became my fayte,
Sucksess I managed on my verray fynalle dayt,
So now, at laste I'm sett to plyght my trothe,
To ye fayre and luvely bisy-nesse wyfe of Howthe.

Ye Philosophre

Ye Philosophre's Tayle

Bye trayde and callinge I'm a philosophre ,
As yett I have no store of golde in Cofre,
But Hopynge for to wynne ye pryze Nobel,
I've lodged myselfe att ye Ashlynge Hotel,
Inn linguage straunge I intereste my mynde,
And note down all ensamples I cann fynde,

Ye linguage spoken straungely on ye Dawrt,
Is sum-thynge that I've taken to my hawrt,
Ye poure manne, middlynge-ryche and well-off,
All utttere voielles in ye mode of Geldof,
Save those who finished schoole awaye in Parys,
And men from Corke who speke lyke Eoghan Harrys.

Summe saye ye Points of Lawger cause ye sound,
Otheres a more empirique raison founde,
They fromm maidens freshe ye accente heare,
And blayme a Syster elocutioneer,
Who hath for manie yeares instructed ille,
Ye laydies yonge above in Syon Hille,

My work, a scientific answere yieldes,
Ye Dawrt disturbs ye Erthe's magnetic fieldes,
For inn ye wyres above ye trayn theyre dwells,
A powrfulle currente thatt awll sensse dispelles,
And those who lyve contiguous to ye Dawrt,
Will foind thurr vurbal mawlecules distawrt.

Ye Wyfe of Bath Avenue

Tara Streete Tayles

Ye Wyfe of Bath Avenue's Tayle

A wydowed wumman five tymes wedde am I,
A lookynge for a manne wyth whome to lye,
Five housbondes have I buryed neathe ye grounde,
And number syx untyl now have nott founde,
Mye eldeste sonne a mariage bureaue runnes,
And bylles me cheep becos I have no funds.

But suitors they cum awk-wardly to hawnde,
For moste of themme they cannot understawnde,
My accente straunge fromm Avenue of Bawth,
Whych causes themm to gyggle and to lawfe,
And in ye pubbe theye quibble and they cawrp,
Whan I demawnd a shawndie made of Hawrp.

I prayed to Gawde sum nyce manne I moite foinde,
Who'd understawnde my accente and my moinde,
I did ye noine forst Froidayes with ye hope,
That a decente, honyste, suitore I'd enrope,
For monthes I lived in deepest dawrk dispaire,
Thynkynge I'd never bee one of a paire.

But nowe ye Lorde hath answered all my prayers,
A manne I have to pylot uppe ye staires,
I mett hym as I journeyed downe ye lyne,
Mye deere, mye swete, my Ludwig Wittgenstein,
He onderstawnds eche everye worde I saye,
Smalle pity 'tis that Wittgenstein is Gaye.

Epilogue

It hath ye strength ye bondes to ondertayke,
Ye Yuppie wyth ye bisy-nesse manne nowe dwells,
Wyth pryde in Wittgenstein ye Wyfe's heart swells,
And reformed Lecher lives with Bisyness-wyfe,
A vybrante happie and contented lyfe.

Of all thys storie's characteres amaine,
One persson lonelie, single dothe remaine,
A yonge man pyning for a partnere dere,
Whose jobbe it ys to couple and to paire,
Ye Bath-wyve's sonne, a poore benyghted ladde,
Who lyves in deepeste, Dartlesse Kinnegadde

AIR ON A G-STRING

Kieran Fagan

MAEVE felt ridiculous. Absolutely and totally ridiculous. She wondered if anyone else knew, could know how ridiculous she felt. The conductor of the choir, an ascetic-looking elderly civil servant by day, patiently coaxing near harmony from an assortment of altos, sopranos and a handful of tenors and basses, surely he could have no suspicion, could he?

In this draughty hall every Monday night for forty weeks of the year, this choir of mostly thirty something, mostly middle-class, mostly women assembled to rehearse.

And the calendar was shedding leaves furiously as the performance date for Carl Orff's Carmina Burana approached. In among the rehearsing sopranos stood the petite form of Maeve, austerely dressed in sensible jumper and skirt and comfortable shoes the very personification of moderate and rational living.

But not only did she feel ridiculous, she was cold too. The hands of the clock on the parish hall wall behind the conductor, Tommy they called him after Sir Thomas Beecham, she supposed, moved agonisingly slowly towards 10pm. A hot whiskey would be just the thing, she thought.

"Going across the road?", she whispered to the woman beside her. Wendy folded her hands below her left cheek and mimed sleep." Early night " she mouthed.

No hot whiskey then. Maeve shivered again. Bloody Peter. It was all bloody Peter's fault. She stamped her foot in annoyance.

Tommy looked up from the score through which he was fumbling. Dear God, he was looking at her. Could he have guessed ? "Did you eh, wish to say something, Mrs eh ahem ?"

Maeve shook her head. "Very well then, we'll just run through the tavern chorus one more time." And as he raised that silly chewed pencil that he used as a baton, Maeve wondered what would happen if she had the courage to tell him and the rest of that smug comfortable crew what was really bothering her.

"Here am I, a respectable married woman, with two children, a cat and a dog and a half-share in a mortgaged semi in a fairly respectable housing estate, just like the rest of you. Except for one thing. My half-wit husband insists on buying my underwear for me."

"Under this sensible woolly jumper and tweed skirt, this respectable mother of two teenage sons is wearing £80 worth of G-string, frilly black suspenders and a bra which is little more than a gauze version of an elastic band. And I'm freezing. Absolutely bloody freezing."

She thought that old Tommy was looking at her again, so she closed her eyes, opened her mouth and soared into the final few bars of the chorus.

But it wasn't Maeve that Tommy was looking at. Wendy was the focus of interest. His eyes had fastened on Wendy's short skirt, or rather on the agreeably plump calves revealed by Wendy's skirt. It was axiomatic among amateur conductors, even of church choirs, that one woman in a short skirt appeared in the front row at all rehearsals.

Male colleagues who gave evening classes reported similar distractions. Most agreed that this was yet another female peculiarity and no significant conclusions could be drawn from it.

This caution was well-founded. Wendy needed a man the way a boxer needs a hungry challenger. The punky spiked red hair, the short leather skirt above thick ribbed tights, were merely the notice outside the gym, inviting the unwary to step inside to have their blocks knocked off.

The final chorus of the tavern scene was eventually whipped into some kind of shape, and the tenors led the charge to the back bar of Culhane's, to put sung theory into blessed practice.

Maeve set off home by car, in that agreeable near-hypnotic state which a good rousing chorus induced in her. Until a twinge of discomfort caused by a particularly nasty piece of stiffened gauze cut into her flesh, brought back the daily realities of Peter's little obsession.

When he used to go into town to work, Maeve could spend her days in a tracksuit and the comfort of sensible items from the underwear counter at Dunnes Stores. But now Peter was home for good, working away on his personal computer in the converted den above the garage. Work came to him now. Great bulky scientific texts swathed in heavily stamped cardboard arrived in green An Post vans throughout the day, and authoritative discussions, analyses, summaries took shape on Peter's flickering screen before being dispatched, via an acoustic coupler, to what Peter called the Mainframe, somewhere on an industrial estate near Shannon airport.

This process did something unhelpful to the telephone line. Wendy and Maeve had been having a good old chat one morning, when the phone just went dead. And the same thing had happened a few days later when Maeve had been trying to make an appointment for a flu vaccination. She'd been so annoyed she rushed into the den.

"Your acoustic whatsit has just cut me off again", she said accusingly.

"Coupler", Peter corrected her automatically. "No it didn't, I haven't used it all day."

Then a guilty look crossed his face and he went over to where the fax machine stood winking busily and started pulling streels of paper that lay on the floor in front of it. "Must have been this", he mumbled, "frightfully sorry."

And he swept up what seemed to Maeve to be page upon page of a Hugh Hefner version of the Janet Reger catalogue on one long crumpled sheet, and tried to stuff it into his desk drawer. Maeve was about to speak, discarded the idea in favour of screaming, then swallowed hard and stamped out.

Not that it made any difference to Peter. Half an hour later he emerged blinking from his den in search of coffee and a chocolate biscuit.

As Maeve stood seething at the kitchen sink, he moved up behind and nuzzled the back of her neck. Her grip on the plastic scourer tightened as she waited for his hands, his cold hands, dammit it was November, to move up under her jumper, as they usually did. But Peter must have sensed her mood because he backed off, stuck the chocolate biscuit in his mouth so he could take another in his free hand and mumbled something about seeing her at lunchtime.

He didn't. She left a cold note taped to the microwave and drove off with a great flourish of squealing tyres to meet Wendy in a Grafton Street department store's salad bar. Among the birch trays and plastic potted plants, Wendy was curiously excited.

"So what do you think I should do about it?" she asked plaintively, as she tried to stuff a wandering spike of hair back into a yellow beret.

"Well", offered Maeve, who had no idea what Wendy was on about but didn't feel the need to say so because all Wendy's conversations were circular, "what do your instincts tell you ?"

Wendy looked sharply at Maeve, as if checking that she was not being made fun of, then said sheepishly, "I'd kill for a slice of that strawberry shortcake."

"So would I, so let's not endanger any more lives, let's just go ahead and order two portions. With cream."

"Oh God, the shame of it."

Later the whole story came tumbling out. "This guy, Lennie, you remember Lennie, he was in our class in school, always very good with his hands..."

Maeve had particular reason to remember Lennie's goodness with his hands, but as Wendy had never suspected anything at the time, there was no reason to burden her now with matters that occured all those years ago.

"Anyway Lennie has moved into the apartment on the ground floor."

"Oh really, isn't that nice. How is he ? Is he married or anything?"

"No I don't think so. You see the problem is he uses his lock-up garage for restoring cars. His garage is right beside mine, and every time I go in and out I see him."

"So why is that a problem ?" Maeve asked, as Wendy's agitation appeared to make a quantum leap.

Wendy looked around anxiously and lowered her voice. "Well, you see, he jacks the car up and rolls in and out on his back on a little trolley."

"So?"

"Every time I go by, he rolls out from under whatever bloody car he's working on and looks up my skirt!" The coffee cup clattered against Wendy's saucer, "And I don't know what you're bloody laughing at either!" she cried in vexation.

Maeve leaned forward and took the clattering cup and saucer out of her friend's hand. So that was why Wendy had forsworn her horrific Doc Martens for the giddy heights of two-inch heels.

"He just finds you attractive, that's all," she murmured to the weeping Wendy. "I expect he's pleased to see you and listens out for your comings and goings."

This cheered Wendy immensely. "Do you think so ?" she sniffed. "You know I always liked him in sixth year, but I got the idea he fancied you."

Maeve shook her head firmly. "Not that I have anything against him," she said firmly, "but no, nothing like that at all." "We were all far too young then," she lied gamely.

By now Wendy was back on top of her form. "I'm so glad I told you Maeve, you're such a dear, and I get into such a muddle. I was even wondering if I should report him for sexual harassment or something like that."

The waitress was hovering, and Maeve stood up to go. Wendy made to do the same, but being as near to crippled by her short skirt and high heels as any able-bodied person can ever be, made heavy going of getting her belongings together.

Then a thought struck her and she pulled at Maeve's arm. "Didn't you say there was something you wanted to talk about, when you phoned...?"

Maeve shook her head firmly, " No, I just fancied a chat, that's all."

"Oh well that's alright then, isn't it ?"

And in a way it was. Though Maeve wished she could just charge off to the ladies like Wendy did. Not that any one would see her of course, but she just felt foolish. What if there was some kind of spy hole in the ceiling to check if people weren't passing drugs in the cubicles, and some great big Ban Garda spotted Peter's latest purchase ? Better get on home as soon as possible.

He was in the kitchen when she returned. "It's not the going into town to work that I miss, it's the lunches," he observed mournfully. "Pity about you" she replied.

"Don't go," Maeve said, "there's something I have to tell you."

Peter put on his best hangdog look.

"Oh you needn't take on like that," said Maeve, "it's just that I've decided to do something about the headboard on our bed." "What's wrong with it?"

"It is horrible, that's what, that off-white quilted stuff with the buttons. I've decided to get one made."

"Right so if that's what you want."

Peter's step was light as he made his way back to the den. He felt that, all things considered, he'd got off lightly.

The next day Maeve visited Lennie. She had a job for him to do. He was surprised to see her, and even more surprised at the nature of her business. It would take about a fortnight, he said, best if she rang him on Monday week. From the searching way he looked at her, Maeve got a feeling that perhaps Wendy had been right about the trolley. It was just as well, perhaps, no there was no perhaps about it, it was just as well that Maeve was wearing trousers.

The next day's postal delivery brought a registered parcel for Peter from a warehouse in Blackburn, Lancashire, if the postmark was to be trusted. By now, Maeve had come to recognise these missives, lighter than the Jiffy bags in which he received his scientific publications.

He gleefully produced two pairs of silk French knickers, one black, one lime green, and was about to suggest that she put on the latter forthwith.

"No chance, Peter. None, not one in the whole wide world." He shrugged and disappeared into the den.

The really strange thing was that for all the fuss he made about things like that, he was not that interested in looking at her wearing them. "Just to know they're there, old girl, that's enough for me," was all he ever said.

French knickers, thought Maeve. It could have been worse, a lot worse. Even though the label said they had been made in Italy. She picked up the black pair and put them away safely. She could put them to good use.

There were, she well knew, worse problems than Peter's harmless fascination with her underwear. There was a young man from Roscommon in her year at UCD who, her friends swore, wore women's frilly pants under his thick corduroy trousers. And she had heard a discussion on Gay Byrne's radio programme about men who liked to dress from head to toe as women.

The thought of Peter's roly-poly form adorned in wisps of satin and gauze had its comic possibilities. Once or twice she thought about bringing matters to a head that way.

"If I must be kitted out like Beryl Cook's fat women picking up bookies' clerks in Plymouth pubs, then you should suffer something similar." But it was no good. He had no interest in wearing anything of hers. Getting rid of a few of his greying pairs of Y-fronts in favour of boxer shorts with red lipstick kisses all over them was as far as she got.

She almost tried to use her mother-in-law in the battle. Not that she could say anything directly to her about it. It would be too shaming. But once, when Peter had gone to collect his mum to bring her over for lunch, Maeve had rushed out to the garden to hang three G-strings and a black and red basque on the clothes line.

Maybe and it was a very faint maybe, Peter could be embarrassed by his mother seeing this colourful and lascivious display.

No chance.

What happened instead was that every male between the age of nine and ninety in the whole of Dublin 14 dropped whatever they were doing to walk up the lane and take a look over her garden fence. Just ten minutes later she rushed out and took them back in again. "Great drying out today, Missus," observed her next-door-neighbour's father, leering cheerfully over the fence. A moment later, Maeve heard Peter and his mother ringing the front doorbell.

The day the headboard arrived was the best day in Maeve's life. She carried it in quietly from the back of the car, managed to get it upstairs without Peter hearing. Lennie had got the measurements absolutely right. It fitted like a glove. And when she plugged it in, the lights came on and glowed most convincingly. With any luck at all, Peter would not see it before bedtime.

At 11pm she went upstairs and had a bath. When he came into the bedroom she was sitting at her dressing table, brushing her hair. "Good God", he said, as he saw the Morris Minor dashboard mounted on a black wood frame, where the headboard of the bed used to be. Lennie had fitted the choke and heater controls. The speedometer glowed in the darkened room. Everything was there, as it had been their first time together that night in the lonely road at the back of the quarry, near Enniskerry, when they had both been students.

There was even a pair of knickers stuffed in the left hand glove compartment. Peter gulped, once, twice, and half sat, half fell onto the bed. Maeve sat down beside him slipped her arm into his. Her dressing gown fell open. She was wearing a navy blue St. Trinians gym slip, trimmed with red, which was many sizes too small for her... Peter gulped again as Maeve unbuttoned his shirt.

Next morning she slipped out of bed before he woke and brought him a cup of tea. He sat up sleepily, gingerly resting his head against the new headboard. "What do you think?" she enquired, "Better than the Morris Minor up at the quarry, eh ?" "More comfortable, anyway where did it come from ?"

Maeve shook her head. "Secret."

"It will have to go, you know. I mean, what if people saw us, I mean it..."

"Like who for example ?"

"Like your friends. Sometimes they leave their coats here when they come for supper.. Wendy and people like that..."

"And your mother."

Peter's face darkened. "Dear God yes, especially my mother, I mean what would she think ?"

"She couldn't have known about what happened up at the quarry", said Maeve.

"Don't you believe it", said Peter vehemently. "She knew about that probably before you did. And the boys too, what would they think, I mean you can't be serious..." He looked anxiously at her, putting down the cup and saucer, and cupping his face in his hands.

"OK, we'll do a deal" said Maeve. "It goes, but with it goes"she pulled out a drawer full of lacy confections, "this lot too." She up-ended the contents of the drawer on the floor.

"Everything" exclaimed Peter, aghast. "Everything" said Maeve, sweeping the mass of black see-through briefs, G-strings, and inhumanly wired mini-bras into the waste paper basket.

Peter nodded gloomily. "I know when I'm beaten."

In the end, Maeve relented a bit. There were one or two pieces she rather liked and these she held on to. For special occasions. And there was an unexpected bonus.

Old Tommy was the first to spot it, the night of the final rehearsal of Carmina Burana. The soprano soloist was giving her all, which in total did not amount to very much, to the dulcissime passage, and the conductor's attention began to wander. "That woman's skirt has got even shorter", he thought to himself.

Then he realised that it was not Wendy's plump thighs which were on view, but Maeve's more delicately arched ones. Wendy had long since relapsed into tracksuits and trainers, fearful that Lenny might take to regarding her as a sex object, rather than an interesting and fulfilled person in her own right.

But Tommy was not to know this. All he could see was a new and smarter, sexier Mrs ahem, Maeve, wasn't that her name ? He looked again.

Then the soloist came to the end of her con abandono passage, and it was time to whip the chorus into action.

"That old goat was looking at my legs", thought Maeve. She had often caught him eyeing Wendy.Now it was her turn and she was just a little shocked to find that Tommy's attention was mildly flattering. Not that she fancied Tommy, but it was nice to be noticed.

And she was being noticed nowadays, more and more. Now that she didn't have to cover up Peter's little purchases, she was able to dress to please herself. And with something warm and sensible underneath, she simply didn't have to cover up from head to toe anymore.

Going shopping in Grafton Street, reading *The Irish Times* over coffee outside the bistro place in the Royal Hibernian Arcade, Maeve looked and became a new woman.

Wendy eyed her "born again" friend with deep suspicion. "If I didn't know you better, I'd think you were having an affair", she muttered grumpily one day. Maeve smiled at her newly-cropped head. For a moment she was on the point of saying "If you knew me better, you'd know that I am. With myself."

But she just continued to smile and said nothing. Often it is better that way. Much much better.

ENDING IT

Padraig O'Morain

DICKIE turned his head and looked at the drinks cabinet he had told Miss Robinson to install the first time he came to work as the boss, the day after his father's burial.

It was the first change he had made in the firm and she had looked solemn and ignored the little joke he had made about it at the time and had given him a dirty look. He remembered the look nearly every time he went near the damn cabinet. Thinking about it made him want a drink right now but he forced himself to put it off.

Wait until this thing is over.

He reached for the telephone and lifted the heavy, black receiver. That would have to go too. It was an old, ugly thing and it belonged to history. He wanted something sleek and modern, which purred softly and didn't jangle harshly and make him jump out of his skin when he was miles away in his mind.

What he would like to get rid of too, while he was at it, was that African mask which, today, seemed to leer at him with more than its usual contempt from its place on the wall beside the door. When Dickie was a schoolboy of eight or nine years, his father had borne it back, under his arm, from a trip to Birmingham and had hung it up on Dickie's bedroom door. That night, after his mother had switched the light out, Dickie, staring nervously at the dark outline of the mask, had become convinced that it was alive. And with the mask hanging on the door, his only means of escape was blocked. He howled for help.

Next morning his father, shaking his head at Dickie's rejection of a present which, as he told the lad, 'any boy would give his eye teeth to have,' tucked the mask back under his arm and brought it off to his office. There he told Miss Robinson to have it hung on the wall. 'It'll make a nice conversation piece.'

Ever since Dickie had moved into the office, after his father's death, the mask had been scowling at him from the wall. He had never felt comfortable with it. You would be sitting there, trying to figure something out, or maybe having a drink to relax, and you would look up and there it would be, staring at you like it knew about everything bad and weak in your mind and loathed you for it. He could have simply got up one day and lifted it off the wall and thrown it in the wastebasket but he had hesitated to do it since it would have meant getting rid of something which had meant something to the old man, and people like Miss Robinson would notice and wonder about it.

With the image of Miss Robinson back in his mind, he stopped thinking about the mask and dialled her extension number on the telephone.

You should have finished it this morning, he said to himself.

He listened to the buzzing at the other end of the line and he almost wished his father was back to handle this business.

'THE thing is,' he had said to Miss Robinson that morning, 'we're going through a bit of a difficult patch.'

She nodded slowly and waited for him to continue. A ghost of a smile touched her lips and Dickie realised that she felt privileged to be called into his office like this and to have a confidence of this gravity imparted to her.

He fought an impulse to look away and stared at her gravely for a couple of moments before continuing. 'Look, you've been with us nearly thirty five years now, isn't that right? You're...almost part of history. The last of the old gang.'

Her smile turned into a little, gloating laugh. A reference to his childhood was on the way.

'I remember the day you were born your father brought in a bottle of Paddy and we sat down in that front office and we drank to your health.' She shook her head as if in wonder. 'He was a proud man that day.'

Dickie let a couple of moments go past and then he took a breath and spoke. 'I was wondering. Have you ever thought of retiring early?'

The smile vanished, her mouth fell open. Her bottom teeth were perfect all the way to the back. Could they be real?

'Fact is, we've got to shed staff,' Dickie said, blushing and feeling as though the words were coming out all awkward. 'And, regrettably, one of our secretaries will have to go. That's why I was wondering if you would think about retiring now.'

Could it be true that George Wilkinson had once had her, on the floor, in front of this very desk? She hadn't looked at all bad when she was younger, according to George. Fifteen, twenty years ago it would have been. If George was telling the truth, he had her, one night, when the building was otherwise deserted, on the carpet in the boss's office, this office, Dickie's father's office – the office with the softest carpet in the house – for a bet because they used to call her The Ice Queen but George reckoned he could have her because he knew she had a crush on him.

Had an awful job shaking her off afterwards, he said. 'Stuck to me like a stamp.' Eventually, so George had said, shakily swirling his umpteenth glass of brandy at his retirement party where he told Dickie the story, he had quietly taken her aside and told her to stop following him around the place. And when she tried to laugh it off, he made his meaning plain by the use of a formula which, he said, had always worked with women: Look, he had said to her laughing face, why don't you just fuck off?

From that day forward she had looked the other way whenever she met him in the corridor or on the stairs and had never spoken to him again, even in the way of business. Whenever Dickie's father gave her a message for George, she would get one of the other girls to deliver it, George had said.

Dickie looked at her glumly for a moment. He couldn't imagine Miss Robinson panting on the carpet. The thing was ridiculous. Marylou, she was called then, of course. His father had called her Marylou until the day he died. But she had become Miss Robinson to everybody else except to the younger secretaries who, resentful of the tongue-lashings she gave them if they came in late or did sloppy work, sometimes referred to her, behind her back, as 'that oul' Robinson bitch.'

She stared at him now, silent and pale.

'You have no commitments, you don't have to worry about supporting anybody,' he said. His voice sounded strained to his ears. 'You'd get by nicely on what you have. You could take your pension early. I got Mr Davenport to work out the figure. You'd get about twenty five quid a week, and you'd have the dole and you haven't far to go to the social welfare pension. And you've got relatives, haven't you, in London? You could pop over and see them whenever you felt like it.'

Silence. Looking at her eyes, he got the impression she was lost in some memory or other. Her face had a solemn look like on the day he ordered the drinks cabinet after his father's funeral. Maybe she was thinking about that.

'Well, I'd like you to think about it because it would be of enormous help to the firm,' Dickie said. He was sweating, and her silence made his nervousness worse. 'And, of course, you'd benefit too. I'll tell you what: let's talk about it again next week.'

She got up and left, without a word, clutching her notebook, and closed the door softly behind her.

Dickie felt disappointed. He had meant to finish her off, get the whole thing over with. Now it was going to drag on into next week. He let out his breath in a long sigh and went over to the drinks cabinet and poured himself a large Jameson.

AFTER Dickie got back from lunch Davenport strolled in, helped himself to a Scotch – Dickie hated the way he did this without asking but since the man had put money into the firm ... He sat on the edge of Dickie's desk and told him about Miss Robinson and the office boy.

It had happened shortly after she left Dickie's office. She had come back to the typing pool from the ladies' toilet to find young Mullins, the office boy, blushing and grinning, in the middle of the room. He usually wore a shirt and jeans but, to Miss Robinson's surprise, he was dressed today in a cheap pinstripe suit which looked a lot like the suit Dickie was wearing. To her mind he looked ridiculous. What age was he? Sixteen?

There were two secretaries in the room. Kate, the young one, was giggling at the boy. The older one, Maura, nearly ten years in the place, was sitting there shaking her head in disbelief.

Miss Robinson glared at the boy but instead of scurrying off as he had always done when she caught him wasting her girls' time, he stood his ground and looked her, grinning, in the eye.

'You can't order me around anymore, Miss Robinson,' he said, exulting, 'I'm being made a trainee manager.'

He laughed and drew another fit of giggles from Kate. 'You better be nice to me now Miss Robinson. I'll be over you before long.'

Miss Robinson struck the boy a blow on the face with the back of her hand.

He swayed under the force of the blow and then he stared at her for a moment in dismay.

'Oh, Miss Robinson!' he said in a shocked voice.

She slapped him on the other side of his face with her open palm.

He yelped and turned and ran out the door.

Kate stared at her with her eyes bulging and her mouth open.

'Good on you, Miss Robinson,' Maura said.

Miss Robinson turned to her a face pale with fury. 'Keep your remarks to yourself,' she said.

Silence returned to the room but for the tat-tat-tat of typewriters as Kate and Maura busied themselves with typing, or pretended to. Miss Robinson sat at her desk, frowning sharply from time to time as if at a bad headache, and turned over the pages of the attendance book for no apparent reason.

DICKIE looked at her solemnly from behind his desk and decided not to invite her to sit down. His stomach was in a knot and he wanted to get this thing over with.

'A senior member of the staff has complained to me about the incident with Terence Mullins,' he recited and then he glanced again at his notes of what Davenport had suggested he say. 'The matter has been considered by myself and by my senior colleagues and I am afraid we cannot allow something like this to happen to a trainee manager.'

'We must take into consideration that he is part of the management team of this company although (Davenport had wanted him to say albeit but he couldn't because it didn't sound real and because he had never said that word before) at the most junior level. If we let this go, what authority would he have in the future not only with yourself but in the eyes of other secretaries? On the other hand, you have been with us for a long time and we don't want to take the sort of step we would normally take in this sort of case.'

She stood quietly, almost blankly. She is waiting, Dickie told himself, for the axe to fall. 'You remember what we talked about this morning?' She nodded.

He cleared his throat and glanced at his notes again. 'I think under the circumstances that it might be a good idea to take it up now. I'm sure I can get the board to agree to the pension in spite of what has happened.' He was tempted to babble on again about how future managers could not be put into a position where secretaries...but he told himself to shut up.

Then he smiled nervously at her just, she recalled, like he had smiled at her once when his daddy had brought him into the office for a visit and Dickie was just a little boy trying not to let on that he was afraid of her. 'It might be as well all round if you went today. In fact, why not take the rest of the day off?'

Her face became a shade more grave. Her eyes stared at him but they seemed empty of emotion. 'If you come in at the end of the week, we'll fix everything up. Or if you like we can post it to you.' He stood and extended a hand. She, in turn, extended a limp, bony hand, as if in a trance, and he shook it. 'We are very grateful to you for all you have done for us and I am sorry that things have ended like this,' he said, noticing, in a distracted sort of way, a smell of talcum powder. 'I'll be asking the board to include a little bonus with your last pay packet.'

He felt a need to soften the blow. He could not think of himself as the sort of man who could do this sort of thing and not give a damn. Suddenly, his eye fell on the mask. 'You know, there is something here which has been with the firm for almost as long as yourself,' he said. He stood and rounded his desk and walked past her to the mask and lifted it off its nail. It was heavier than he expected. He held it out to Miss Robinson. 'I'd like you to have it.'

She took the long, polished, heavy mask and looked from its scowling face to Dickie's frightened face. She spoke in a voice he could hardly hear. 'Is that all?'

'Yes, that's all and goodbye and thank you.'

And then he was alone in his office, heart thumping, sweat running down his face and giddy with elation.

True to Type

HE raised the glass. Damn fine glass. Good and heavy, you could feel money in its heaviness. This was his second visit to the drinks cabinet since Miss Robinson had left his office. The first drink was to celebrate the end of the day's ordeals and the second was the first drink of the evening. Dammit, he had earned the right to start early. How many men had done the things that he had done today and it not yet four o'clock?

He held the glass up to catch the light from the window and, as he did so, Miss Robinson walked into view on the street below, in her raincoat, and with a shopping bag in one hand and a handbag in the other. She kept her eyes on the ground and her shoulders were a little hunched.

Under one arm was the long, wooden mask. Its empty eyes glared sideways at the passing traffic. Then it began to slip and she stopped and put down the shopping bag and tucked the mask more firmly under her arm and picked up the bag again and walked on.

The last of the old crowd, Dickie said to himself, suddenly feeling sentimental.

She walked on and was hidden by traffic as she trudged toward whatever destiny awaited her.

Behind him, a door opened.

Goodbye Marylou, he said in his mind before he turned to see who was there.

SPACE INVADER

Fergus Brogan

JAMES lay on the warm stones of the pebble beach and idly watched the windsurfers falling into the water. Parents were shouting not to go out too far; neurotic dogs were barking at the waves; radios were screaming that Galway had only two minutes left and a group of frisbie throwers were producing loud peals of girly squealing. But the sun was warm and James felt pleasantly disposed towards the world.

A young woman protruding in all the right directions from a yellow bikini stepped over him and retrieved the plastic disc – for the third time. Her friends doubled in convulsive giggling.

James lay back and twiddled his toes in the warmth. His mind was running over the possibility of conducting experiments in dexterity on people with different degrees of opposed thumb, for James was a keen anthropologist. He raised his thumb and forefinger against the sun and squinted at the angle unaware of a fresh outburst of suppressed giggles. He had just deduced that a dexterity test would require examinations of strength, speed and sensitivity when the yellow bikini tripped over his leg.

"Sorry" it said.

"My fault entirely" he apologised, drawing in his long legs and raising himself uncomfortably on one elbow, to face an athletic young woman.

"You shouldn't lie there for too long, if you're not used to the sun" she offered, rubbing her wet thighs with a towel, "you could get badly burned."

In a rare flash of repartee James replied: "You're obviously well used to it".

True to Type

He was very pleased with himself as bantering with young women was a form of communication in which he was totally incompetent. It emboldened him to steal a glance at the golden curve above the bikini bottom which was now being dabbed with exaggerated care.

"Cheek" she said ambiguously, and with mock modesty wrapped herself in the towel

James was not a man used to the company of women. In fact the only woman he had ever really touched in his 25 years, apart from his mother – and that was unavoidable – was a young *homo erectus pekinensis* and he had only discovered that she was female after extensive measurement of the pelvic cradle. But this young woman was different – more flesh for one thing – and she was definitely upsetting his centre of gravitas.

She sat on her towel facing him and folded her legs about her. She seemed genuinely enthusiastic in his opposed thumb project, though she didn't know a great deal about it, but would love to learn more. She wondered if his wife minded him leaving all those old bones lying around the house. He hadn't got a wife. She supposed his flatmates must be very difficult to get along with when he was studying. He lived alone. She imagined buying a house must be very expensive nowadays. He had a good salary from the institute, and anyway, he quipped, as he nervously entered a conversation charged with pre-sexual tension "happy mortgages are made in heaven".

By the time she left him – she had written "Anne-Marie 954859" in eye pencil on his wrist – he was in a state of high excitement.

THEY met the next Friday, had a very nice evening, chatted about this and that, enjoyed the French film – which she felt sure he would like – and the drink afterwards and parted with an arrangement for the following week. There was not the slightest hint of overt sexuality in anything that was said or done.

Within three weeks they were lovers. They spent hours holding and touching. He fondled her golden curves and they laughed about the day on the beach. They wrapped themselves in the sheets, made strange meals of eggs and tea and stale bread and always returned to bed to make love and gaze at each other.

A SHORT time afterwards James observed strange growths in his bathroom. Tubes sprouted overnight and strange lotions mushroomed along the window-sill. Packets, unguents, oils and salves took hold in the medicine chest and flimsy pink things grew down form the shower-rail. James grew very nervous, and with good cause, for when his mother called, he had to leave her ringing the bell while he rushed about hiding things.

Anne-Marie, he realised, was marking out her territory; it reminded him of the tribal rites of the Aurignacians of the upper Elbe who urinated around the perimeters of their camp-sites.

In the succeeding months Anne-Marie developed the habit of calling to his job for coffee – she was now on first-name terms with all his colleagues – and occasionally she surprised him in the lounge bar where he went for lunch.

When she lost her flat – the landlord's sister was moving back in – she was quite distraught. She just couldn't go home to her family because her mother knew all about them.

The logic of this escaped James, so he let it pass, but he did try to resist the inevitable. "My cousin Roger. . . you know the one I told you about . . . is coming home from Zambia soon and will need a place with privacy . . . he plays the trombone . . . I told you that . . . and maybe, probably, I was thinking that here would be . . ."

Her head turned slowly like the turret on a Sherman tank, bringing her large-calibre black eyes to bear on him. The unspoken cannonshell of contempt blew him into a thousand pieces.

She drove him from the kitchen, fought him across the living-room and inflicted heavy casualties in the bedroom. After that, there was some minor resistance and occasional outbreaks of guerrilla activity. Then she ran her frilly things up the clothesline in full view of the neighbours and the fortress fell.

She moved her stuff in "officially" at the end of the month and a succession of friends and relatives (including the mother who knew *all*) came to help her "put things right". Mother left toilet-cleaner and washing-up liquid and her friend Imelda left more little jars for the bathroom window-sill.

Anne-Marie was thrilled and made a special curry – their first real meal at home together, she called it. She chatted on excitedly unaware of his blackening mood. Nobody could say that Mother had not been civil about things, she suggested and James, who wasn't quite sure what these "things" were and why anybody should have any right to be uncivil about anything, foolishly agreed that nobody in her right mind, which category could hardly include her mother, could say that. Bitter word followed bitter word and after a tearful scene, Anne-Marie went up to bed and locked the bedroom door.

Alone in the his kitchen, James began to feel once more the glow of privacy. He made himself a special salad putting in all the things she didn't like – red cabbage, hot peppers, French dressing and lots of garlic. Then with three-quarters of a bottle of wine, he watched several Open University programmes – she preferred Nighthawks – and slept soundly on the sofa.

When he returned from work the next evening her friend Imelda was sitting in his chair, drinking coffee from his Magdalanian beaker, the one he had brought back from the dig in Antwerp. The remorse he had been feeling during the day turned to rage. It was the last straw. He had been put upon, invaded, his privacy and his way of life taken from him. He would stand it no more . . .

WHENEVER she goes for a stroll on the pebble beach, Anne-Marie shows the children the place where where their father first asked her out.

THE CANTILEVER PRINCIPLE

Mary Morrissy

"TRUSSED-UP," my father was saying, "like a chicken. Oven-ready!"

He beamed at me, grateful for my indulgence – I had heard the story several times over – then turned back to Sam.

"They daubed this stuff on me, like washing-up liquid. Rubbed it on neat – all over!"

"By the prettiest nurse, no doubt, Jack!" Uncle Sam winked extravagantly. They were like boys again, gleeful with reprieve. Sam, snowy-haired, with a grizzled jaw, and my father, propped up on the pillows, his face ripe and waxy as a windfallen apple. The danger had passed. We were safely allowed our gaiety. Indeed, it was necessary because we had so nearly lost him. We lost my mother – early. For years he had measured time by her death. That was, he would say, puckering his brow, that was just before we lost your mother. That was his word for it. Lost.

I cannot remember her now except as a collection of sensations cut adrift – the smell of cold cream, the steady thump of another heart, a benign shape leaning over me as a prelude to embrace. He was generous with details of her. They had met at a tea dance at the Metropole. She was a good deal younger than him. He had been accused of cradle-snatching. They had walked out together for eight months. Her family did not approve. After they were married his landlady let her move in. Then there was the flat by the canal before they bought a home – here. This other world that they belonged to, grey and grainy, the one before I was born, this was where I was convinced my mother was lost. I identified the year as 1947, the worst winter on record, and pictured her wandering in a blizzard in the wrap-around coat and angora beret she wore in those long-ago holiday snaps. These seemed always to be taken in winter, at the edge of cliffs, my mother's hair wild around her face, her teeth chattering with cold through a brave smile. My father, it has to be said, looks pretty goofy in these pictures. The short-back-and-sides haircut, his large ears, a gormless sort of smile. He has improved with age. Whereas she seems perfect then, for then, as if she somehow knew...but, no, that's ascribing premonition to mere candour for the camera.

Of her death he would not speak. A brain haemorrhage. My only guide is Mrs Parfitt. He had left for work. And where was I? Somewhere out of the picture. She is sitting over the debris of breakfast things. It is a wan April morning aching to be spring. She is gazing out the kitchen window, elbows propped on the table, one hand clasping a cup of lukewarm tea. Suddenly there is an intruder who strikes her one blow on the temple sending everything spinning. The cup leaps from her hand, a plate slides off the edge of the table. She tries to rise but her arm buckles beneath her, crumpling the waxed folds of the oiled cloth and rattling the teapot. Her last view is of the mocking darkness of its spout. My father finds her at lunchtime, face bathed in milk, crumbs in her hair, dried blood around her ear. He thinks she has passed out or, comically, has fallen asleep.

He leaves her be and calls a neighbour – the inner workings of women are no business of his. *She* knows.

"She's dead, Mr Eustace," Mrs Parfitt says, "your wife is dead." Here, she says, here at this very table.

WITHOUT a mother, not only death, but birth, too, was a mystery. We found you in a basket on the canal, my father used to say. I liked the "we" in this; for the first time it included me. And it beat those stories about cabbage leaves. I could imagine this. The pair of them walking along the tow-path near the gasworks and finding a Moses basket in the green, scummy water by the bank. My mother (wearing the same hat and coat; there are no costume changes for her) lifts me out carefully.

"Ah look," she says, "look at the wee mite."

I am wearing a long white christening robe.

"John, just look."

She hoists me up on her shoulder and turns around so that he is looking directly into my eyes. Was it then it started – this fierce, reluctant attachment?

She swings around, her voice brimming with excitement and says: "Shall we keep her?" as if it's the most reckless, daring adventure they have ever considered.

My father says yes.

HOSPITAL time is different. Elongated. It was – is – high summer but already the recent gusty, blue-bright days and cool, lilac evenings belong to a carefully delineated past. Even the heartbreaking sunsets, melancholy and grand, which accompanied my vigil, now seem like the fevered reproduction of some long distant memory. A by-pass. Appropriate surgery for the man. My father, the engineer. Bridges were his thing. During school holidays we made pilgrimages to them. I remember a misty January evening standing reverentially by the Forth Bridge which rose like a giant brontosaurus out of the still waters.

"The cantilever principle," my father said importantly. "See, the three spans." He pointed, one hand on my shoulder. "They each stand separately but when projected towards each other they form a bridge. Stress against stress."

I WAS terrified that he would die.

"Don't worry," Sam had said," he's a hardy one."

But the warning signs, once glimpsed, will never go away. His breathlessness, the alarming puce of his cheeks, the panic in his eye. I had seen them all and knew the cold, hard dread they induced in me. I grew to hate him for his frailty. I despised him when he gasped for air. I turned away, ashamed, when he clutched his chest in pain. I told myself he was pretending, doing it for effect, and that sympathy would only make him weaker. He had deceived me. His robust good health all these years had been a sham. He had secretly been cultivating the germ of his own death.

INTENSIVE Care. My father adrift somewhere while all around him gadgets did his struggling for him. There was a bleeping green monitor and the noisy shuffling of a ventilator. Narrow tubes snaked in under the bedclothes and a bulbous bag of intravenous drip stood sentry at the bedhead. It reminded me of the pictures of bridges he collected, all huge beams and girders and in between the steel and metal latticework, a tiny train trapped.

The hardware hid him from me; all his fear and helplessness put on hold.

"It's quite normal," one of the nurses assured me, "we keep them heavily sedated. Lessens the likelihood of rejection."

For days I sat by his bedside or paced up and down the phlegm-coloured corridors. The light there was dull and dead as if it, too, had been etherised. And the noise – like the muted clamour of a penitentiary. The wheeling and droning of cleaners, the rattle of trolleys shivering with instruments, the clangour of bed pans gave way to periods of forsaken quiet. At night, after visiting hour, it seemed as if we were on board a ghostly liner, abandoned and adrift. Sometimes I would go to the Day Room. A television with the sound turned down was perched high on a ledge. Animated faces on the screen mouthed messages to the silent room. Several patients would be slumped in the leatherette armchairs which broke wind when they sat down. Their slippers chafed the shiny lino. Some of them had crude crosses in gentian violet daubed on their faces to mark where they'd been treated. It was also a cancer hospital.

That must have been what he had. My friend. That's what I thought of him as, although we never spoke. He was in the ward opposite the intensive care unit, his bed just inside the door. He was a young man, the same age as me, perhaps. He lay on the bed in pyjama bottoms and a dressing gown, open and stranded around his waist. There was, to look at him, no sign of illness except for the shaved rectangle at his temple. Beneath the hurtful ridge of his brow his eyes were sunken, fogged-looking, slow to register, and yet, I had the feeling that I was being watched intensely. He was stricken on one side. Above his head like a noose, a tubular triangle hung. With one arm he used this to manoeuvre himself in the bed. He moved his good leg constantly, grinding his heel against the bed-clothes like the restless kicking of a baby. Everything about him was like a baby. The awful trustingness of his gaze. The little identity tag around his wrist with those bare details with which he had come

into the world – his name, his date of birth. He seemed utterly de-
fenceless and alone.

And yet, he was not alone. A woman, Miriam, (I gave her a name,
but never him) came daily, kissing him on the forehead before set-
tling down in a chair beside his bed. She moved with what seemed
like exaggerated care as if any sudden gesture might startle him. He
watched her silently, following her about wonderingly with his eyes.
He would grasp her hand, rubbing his fingers on her knuckles as if
touch were new to him. I could hear her speak soothingly to him.

Intimacy is shocking in a hospital, absurd amidst the starch and
clatter, and *their* tenderness, especially, seemed alien. But I couldn't
take my eyes off them. She drew things from a crowded tote bag like
a conjurer desperate to please. She brought flowers which she carefully arranged in a jug beside the bed. Once she sellotaped a child's
drawing to the side of his locker. She fed him, handing him a cup
with a straw in it to drink from. She wiped his mouth. She peeled
fruit for him – oranges, bananas – holding them up in front of him
before clamping his fingers firmly around them. It was like watching a mother and child. I felt as I do when women breastfeed in
public. The fear of other people's nakedness.

I NEVER wanted to know any more about him except what I could
learn from watching. Perhaps I knew the bargain I was about to
make. His life for one I valued more.

"And at last Pharaoh made a proclamation to the whole of his
people: Whenever a male child is born, cast it into the river, keep
only the girls alive. And now one of the descendants of Levi wooed
and married a woman of his own clan, who conceived and bore him
a son. So winning were the child's looks that for three months she
kept him hidden away; then, unable to conceal him any longer, she
took a little basket of reeds, which she smeared with clay and pitch,
and in this put her baby son down among the bulrushes on the river
bank..."

ON the third day there was a change in my father's condition. I de-
tected this only by a certain change in the atmosphere, an added
grim bustle in the room. The nurses, usually chatty and given to
small talk, conferred with one another instead at the door casting

anxious glances in my direction. They made what seemed to be futile adjustments to the equipment, picked up my father's lumpen hand to get a pulse with an air of resignation, leafed through his charts as if searching for some clue to his condition they'd overlooked. I didn't ask them, of course, what they thought was wrong. I was too afraid. "Not responding," was a phrase I overheard.

Meanwhile in the ward opposite, my friend was celebrating. He was in a wheelchair by the bed, a rug thrown over his legs. Above him, hanging from the curtain rails was an array of balloons and streamers, and Miriam was stringing together a loop of cards behind his bed. It was his birthday. In the afternoon visiting hour, a gang of people arrived. They drew up in a circle around him. Some perched on the bed, others stood. There was the popping of corks and a rush of paper cups to catch the foaming champagne. There were bursts of raucous laughter, an air of triumph.

"Come on," someone called out to one of the nurses, "join the party!"

"Ye'll all be thrown out," she warned mockingly.

A loud "awh" from the group.

I couldn't see him in the midst of them but I imagined him there smiling jaggedly, drunk with memory. When the visitors' bell rang at four they wheeled him recklessly out of the ward and down the corridor towards the Day Room, whooping and singing – "Happy birthday to you, happy birthday to you, happy birthday dear..." The swing doors closed behind them.

THREE a.m. Condition, stable. They had told me to go home but I wouldn't. I didn't trust them. I was a nuisance, I knew that, prowling around, nervously alert from lack of sleep and haunted by unspoken fears. Even Sam had got irritated.

"Don't do the martyr on us. For God's sake, go home. There's nothing you can do here," he had said when he left at midnight. He was right; there *was* nothing I could do – there or anywhere else. But I thought that any sudden movement of mine might precipitate disaster. As long as I was there, nothing could happen to him.

There is something sacred about those early hours of the morning. A hush. It isn't difficult to see why death comes then, how it gains easeful entry when the defences of the world are down. The graveyard hours. If Dad makes it through these, I thought, he will make it through another day. It was then I remembered my friend. I slipped out of Intensive Care and crossed the corridor. He too was sleeping. It was a warm night and he had thrown off all the bedclothes except for a sheet swaddled around his groin. In the blue light his limbs looked startlingly beautiful; there were perfect half-moons on all his fingernails.

A breeze sighed softly at the open window. I thought of wind among rushes. It would be easy now to push him forth out into the calm waters of the night in this, the easeful hour. I laid my hand on his pillow. There would be no struggle. In his slumber he would barely notice the gentle rocking of the basket. He was the boy-child, the one who must be sacrificed. And, in return, my father would be saved. Take him, I urged the darkness, take *him*.

BY the next morning my father was awake, in a different ward, the hardware all removed. He smiled sheepishly at me as I came in, as if he'd been away on a drunken binge.

"I'm sorry," he said weakly, "for giving you a fright."

"You had us worried, you old dog," Sam said," we'd thought you'd given up the ghost. Isn't that right, Kate?"

For days, almost a week, I dared not see my friend. It was easy to avoid him. His ward was on the floor below and I did not have to pass it now. Only when my father could leave his bed did I have the courage to venture down. I walked along the familiar corridor, halting at his doorway. The bed was empty, the locker cleared. The child's drawing had been torn roughly from its spot leaving only a corner scrap. The coverlet on the bed did not even bear the outline of his body.

"Gone, my dear," a nurse said as she bustled past.

I did not – could not – ask what she meant by gone.

I WATCH out for him on the street now. Certain men remind me of him. I see them in pubs, on trains, in buses, and my heart leaps. I am about to rush up to them when they turn around and reveal themselves as impostors.

Anyway, I know it's all in vain. I know the price that's been exacted. I *know* that I will never see him again.

WHITE SPACE

Deaglán de Bréadún

IT WAS getting late. The last pages would have to be off the stone soon, to allow the country edition to be printed. If the paper wasn't ready in time for the train to Cork there would be big trouble.

Syl was more than anxious to get the job finished so he could slip across the road to Flaherty's for an after-hours pint and a whiskey. "I like to keep my hands busy," he'd say with a chortle to the other late-night topers. Meanwhile his boss, Jeremy, was getting into a flap: that guy was forever losing his cool. "If you can keep your head when all about you are losing theirs and blaming it on you. . ." You got these headless chickens on every newspaper, but the *Chronicle* seemed to have more than its fair share.

"Main sports page headline too short," said Jeremy, who always spoke in North of England telegraphese at the sharp end of the night. He looked pale and flustered, a one-ulcer man in a two-ulcer job. Syl wondered if Jeremy knew that "Clenched Hair" was his nickname in the caseroom. "Be hell to pay tomorrow if paper's late again," Jeremy said.

Syl took a look at the main headline on the sports page. Shy by a mile: if that got through they'd be a laughing-stock. The late sports sub who should have been looking after the page was nowhere in sight.

Syl's thoughts of revenge were rudely interrupted as Jeremy thrust a galley proof into his hand. "C'mon, write heading that fills bloody line," he snapped.

I suppose I'd better see what the story is about, said Syl to himself, recalling fondly for a moment the Fleet Street old-timer who boasted of never reading the copy he subbed.

It was a preview piece on that day's Grand National. "Bootboy may score" was the headline. There was a long, rambling introduction and the tipster didn't actually mention Bootboy until the last paragraph. Just before that, however, there was a reference to the 25-to-1 outsider, Afghan Warrior, as "potential value for money."

"Get a move on, for crying out loud," someone roared in his ear. No time to lose. Afghan Warrior's name instead of Bootboy's in the headline would kill a lot of that embarrassing white space. All he had to do then was cut out the last paragraph with its reference to Bootboy. This would create a small hole but there were plenty of fillers handy. No doubt the author of the piece would be furious at the distortion of his work, but how was he to know who rewrote the headline? This was no time for the niceties of conscience. Besides, the guy should have mentioned Bootboy in the intro.

Syl's instructions were carried out and the paper put to bed at last. The drama and the pain always reminded him of a mother giving birth. The caseroom, which moments before had the atmosphere of a wrestling-match, suddenly grew quiet as the men slipped away in twos and threes for a discreet pint of ale or stout.

As always, the tension drained out of Syl the minute he sat up on his favourite barstool in the back snug of Flaherty's. The break was only for 20 minutes but he put away his usual quota of two pints and a double whiskey in that time. One of the old-timers on the *Chronicle* was extolling the purity of the paper's traditional hot-metal production methods over the vulgar new computer technology coming in everywhere else. A fierce argument broke out, then stopped abruptly when the landlord threatened to close the bar. Syl went back to the paper to see the city edition through. Then, his mind too active for sleep, he headed for a shebeen on the other side of town to kill the remaining hours until dawn.

His fellow-drinkers were a mixed bunch: some came from other papers and there was a smattering of taxi-drivers, waiters and actors, as well as one or two off-duty policemen whose presence ensured that the place would not be raided. There was lino on the floor and the proceedings were supervised by an elderly widow who took care to exclude ladies of the night. There was a legend that in her younger and hardier days she had "bounced" Brendan Behan for obstreperous behaviour. Everyone treated her with a wary respect.

Well-oiled though he was, Syl kept a discreet silence as the others expressed surprise at his paper's choice of Afghan Warrior to win the Grand National. True, the prize at Aintree often went to a rank outsider but there were usually so many of these you had great difficulty picking the likely nag. It was useless relying on tips in the papers—you were as well off using a pin.

"Maybe he knows something," one of the boys said eventually. His argument was that a tipster writing about a big race for a national daily would hardly stick his neck out like this without good reason . The majority took the view that the writer was "off his rocker". Syl winced as he listened to the conversation. He knew when he wrote the headline about Afghan Warrior that it had been a bit tenuous but in the heat of the moment he thought he would get away with it. Now the words "potential value for money" came back to haunt him. Obviously all the writer had meant was that the horse was a good each-way bet with just a remote possibility it might take first place. But the real tip for the day had of course been Bootboy. Syl groaned: why hadn't he thought of changing the headline again for the city edition? There had been some rejigging to do on the front page and it had driven all thoughts of horses from his mind.

He now realised that there would be ructions over his headline. He could picture the scene as Jeremy and himself were arraigned in MacConachie's office. Although he affected the airs of a gentleman, especially since he was appointed Editor, MacConachie's bullying nature was never far from the surface. "What kind of moron are you to write that bloody headline," he would roar, as Syl cowered before him. Then, turning on poor, ulcer-ridden Jeremy: "What was going on in that peanut-sized brain of yours when you let it through?" On and on it would go, MacConachie's Donegal accent getting thicker as he worked himself into a rage. It wouldn't end there: for weeks afterwards they would be targets for acid and sarcastic comments, in the corridors, in the caseroom, at editorial conferences. And all because of a split-second decision...

"What's the matter Syl? Bored with all this talk about the gee-

gees?" The mocking, friendly face of George O'Brien was leering at him across the table.

Syl said nothing. George was a good mate but not to be completely trusted. He would tell the whole world the yarn about the headline, not out of malice but just for the sheer pleasure of watching Syl squirm with discomfort.

The dawn's uncompromising light after the darkness of the shebeen was always a shock. A few of the lads were moving on to one of the "early houses", the market pubs with special permission to open ahead of the rest. Usually Syl accompanied them but it had been a hard night so he took a taxi home instead.

When they got to his home the driver had to shout to wake him. The house was cold and forbidding: for a moment he thought he heard knocking at the back door, but he saw nobody when he went to investigate. His watch had stopped, so he rang the talking clock. "At the signal it will be seven forty-three and forty seconds," the anonymous voice told him. Syl realised he had no-one else to talk to. He lurched up the stairs and sank into bed.

He dreamt that there was a wild horse in the back garden. All of a sudden, the horse was transformed into a rough, violent youth with a skinhead haircut and heavy boots who was kicking the door down. "Bootboys rule OK!" the youth was screaming. "I'm going to smash your bleeding head in!"

Just as the bootboy was coming through the back door Syl escaped in a taxi. But when the driver turned around he had Jeremy's face. "Made right cock-up of sports page," Jeremy's mouth was creased in contempt. "Afghan bloody Warrior. . . be lucky if we get jobs in Kabul when this is over." Syl pleaded with Jeremy to keep his eyes on the road, but it was too late. The car skidded and was hurtling towards the wall of the newspaper building where they both worked...

Syl woke up drenched in sweat. A gnome was operating a jackhammer inside his head. Have to take the pledge, he said to himself. The time had come round for another futile gesture.

Men like Syl are frequently married but, almost as frequently, their wives have left them in despair. There was no-one to have lunch with at home, so he wrapped a coat around him and ventured out in the rain to the local for some pub grub. All the talk was about the 'National and even Syl with his constitutional aversion to sport of all kinds found himself being drawn into the excitement.

In the middle of it all a news bulletin came on the television. The main item concerned the war in Afghanistan. Syl paused, his glass at his lips. Afghanistan! He was not a great believer in signs and portents, but maybe he should have a bet on that old nag after all. Some things were meant to be.

He nipped into the bookie's shop next door and laid out three tenners to win on Afghan Warrior, still at 25-to-one. What the hell, it was only money.

Syl had reached the age when he thought there would be no more excitement in his life, but the 'National turned out to be gripping stuff. Bootboy had taken the lead early on but fell at Becher's Brook. Coming up to the last fence, Syl's horse was in second place and as it began to close on the leader in the home stretch, Syl found himself shouting, "Come on Afghan Warrior! Come on, ya boy ya!"

Afghan Warrior won the race by half-a-length. The regular punters, well aware of Syl's lack of interest in the horses, kept a monastic silence as he raised the rafters with a cheer. They brightened up a little when he bought them a drink. Most of them had plumped for Bootboy. "I was only following the tip in my own paper," said Syl with malicious pleasure. "I don't know why you guys bother with the English tabloids." He could hardly wait to meet Jeremy at work that night.

Someone was working out how much Syl had won. "Thirty by twenty-five is, hold on, seven hundred and fifty lids. Mother of God!"

"Easy come, easy go," said Syl as a huge tray of drinks arrived. He lifted a big, creamy pint off the tray and held it high in the air.

"Here's to working in newspapers," he said. "More vitamins than any other job."

STRIKING HOURS

Paddy Woodworth

Denak dute golpatzen. Azkenak dute hiltzen.

I HAD found these words carved into a clocktower in a graveyard, in a little village about 20 miles inland from the French Basque coast. I had no idea what they meant, but they seemed like a motto I had found beneath another clock in a similar graveyard just across the Pyrenees in Navarre. Phrases seem more memorable in languages you don't understand, and the words had stuck in my mind, like a comforting mantra or a child's nonsense rhyme.

Then they caught my eye again, in yet another village cemetery, and this time Xabier was with me. He had Basque from birth, and had mastered most of the obscure dialects of that most obscure language as well.

We were in the graveyard that time because we were waiting for the sound man to set up in the church which was, as usual, the only venue where Xabier could play his folk songs in the small villages where he was a popular guest artist at fiestas. The priests, on both sides of the border, were often Basque nationalists who turned a blind eye to Xabier's total indifference to religion and the distinctly secular and occasionally bawdy songs he sang. Besides, they probably argued with themselves, his concerts brought young people into the church who hadn't been there since they were baptised.

The other times? Well, I'm not religious, and certainly not morbid. It was just that the villages are small and I often ended up wandering into the cemetery. It usually lay perched outside the boundaries of both the village and the church, because Basque superstition about the dead is stronger than Basque Christianity. The new religion came very late to the Northern Pyrenees. Look at the way the ancient solar motifs outnumber the crosses on the little headstones if you don't believe me - or look at the records of the Spanish inquisition.

The little stone hamlets of Navarre were a target-rich environment for the priests with long white faces and red-hot irons who came up from the South in search of heretics and witches. Christianity was always only skin-deep in the Basque Country, though the withered old herbalists and fresh young peasant girls whom the inquisitors tortured and burned undoubtedly had more love in their hearts than their tormentors ever had. Not that love has counted for much, wherever the shadows of Rome and Geneva have fallen.

I digress. But not too far, I think, because the story I want to tell will end in another graveyard, and there will be sin and inquisition and yes, torture also, before the end. And there will be love, a love borne patiently, inscribed on a face which the motto on the clocks at once called to my mind.

"It means," said Xabier, enjoying his occasional role as interpreter of the cryptic ways of his people, "that ...all hours strike, but the last one ...kills. This is true, don't you think?" He spoke the translation with deliberate hesitation for dramatic emphasis, and added his commentary with a note of ironic complicity.

We were both getting close enough to 40 to insure instinctively against encroaching age by the occasional wry acknowledgement of time's winged chariot's passage; we were still far enough away from 50 to be able to banish the chill of those wingbeats with the heat of a single cognac or a single glance returned meaningfully by a hot young woman . I didn't feel that most of the hours had hit me that hard anyway, and I didn't want to think about the last one. I couldn't help thinking, though, of the face of the woman who had served me unseeingly in a familiar bar the previous night.

IT wasn't the first time she had served me, not by a long chalk. Senora Etxebeste must have been about 35 , I suppose, when I saw her first, in 1978, and she had then carried her age with confidence and grace, though hardly beauty. Her husband, five years older perhaps, looked prematurely lined and often seemed a little harassed. Maybe they had already over-extended themselves on the borrowing for the decoration of the bar, which was still gleaming in those days, in all its pristine modern luxury. I remember that there was always fragrant soap in the dispensers in the toilets, at a time when most bars in the village didn't even bother with a washhandbasin for their customers.

If they had overspent, that didn't seem to worry Senora Etxebeste: she had her three lovely children, and they were more than enough to confirm the essential benevolence of life. I didn't know about the third one, then, of course, or, if I did, I don't remember. It was the two elder ones who had made an impression.

Jon was goodlooking, with a sunny, open smile and strong brown eyes. I suppose he was about 16. He used to carry the postprandial coffees, cognacs and cigars to our table, which had a view of the vertiginous green valley below the village. He always carried them held high on a shining silver tray, as though he was a waiter in one of the swanky bars in central Bilbao, but he didn't take the role very seriously. His levity was betrayed in the way he swayed easily to the bar's superior muzak - Dire Straits or Pink Floyd - as though he were serving guests in his own apartment. He never let anything fall, though. He laughed a lot, often in self-mockery and never, that I saw, in malice.

You could see that he was the centre of the *cuadrilla*, or circle of friends, who used to return to the bar again and again in the course of an afternoon or evening. There were usually about ten of them, with fringe members who would drop in and out. Mostly they were boys, some of them with fancy motorcycle leathers, and the few girls were dressed in the tight black jeans and long shapeless green anoraks that were fashionable that year.

They were still too young to form couples publicly, and generally avoided physical contact between the sexes, though the boys were constantly embracing, leaning on each other or punching each other playfully. But the sexual revolution was trickling into the Basque villages, and the air around the *cuadrilla* was sometimes heavy with desire. Every so often, a boy and girl would take off on a moped, chased down the narrow street out of the village by the lewd comments of their friends. Somehow, they never came back together, or so it seemed to me. Jon watched the comings and goings with good humour, never able to participate because he was always working.

Occasionally you could sense a friction between Jon and his father, perhaps because Jon's *cuadrilla* was so often clustered around the bar, and spent so little money. The girls mostly drank tonics, only adding gin to their drinks late in the evenings, and the boys knocked back the cheapest red wine or tiny *zurritos* of beer, mere thimblefuls. Like I said, Senor Etxebeste had appointed his bar with considerable comfort, with floppy leather armchairs and smart white tables, to attract young professionals with money to spend.

The young professionals from Bilbao were commonplace now, but Senor Etxebeste could remember how strange and alien they had seemed when they first appeared, back in the early 1960s. For the older people in the village, some of whom had never been down to the main road, Bilbao was Sodom and Gomorrah, seething with Spanish immigrant workers who spouted atheistic socialism and spent their free time in brothels. At first, the newcomers were regarded with a suspicion close to hostility, a hostility which their zealous but halting attempts to communicate in a bland, urban dialect of Basque did nothing to alleviate.

The first group to come regularly were a group of alpinists, refurbishing an old house as a base for weekend mountaineering expeditions. They had the seriousness of their hobby, and some of them had an added gravitas born of stern and risky political commitment. Somebody saw two of them training with pistols once, deep in the woods above the village, the word got around, and the next weekend the place was crawling with Guardia Civil. Not the lazy, happy, corrupt guardias who did deals with the smugglers who used the high mountain paths, but Franco's representatives on Earth, real animals. There were the usual arrests and the usual crude tortures. A village boy, Txomin Garaikoetxea, who had innocently acted as a guide for the outsiders, was dumped back at his parent's door from a police jeep. He had a damaged eye and swollen testicles. Nobody was happy that the outsiders had brought trouble with them, but they were respected now.

In the years to come, Txomin would swim the Bidasoa river to the relative sanctuary of France, where, rumour had it, he quickly became the person in charge of all ETA operations involving the safe passage of commandos across the border. His doting grandmother, who lived in a *caserio* outside the village, kept some Parabellum pistols in a leather bag in her cattle byre, until two guardias found them. They shot her in the legs, stripped two of her teenage grand-daughters to the waist, and forced them to drag her dying body on a hand-cart through the village.

The next wave of young Bilbainos to hit the village had a less dramatic impact, though they, too, would alter its way of life, eventually beyond recognition. First a luxury apartment block started going up, ugly and incongruous, at the edge of the village, and Senor Etxebeste heard the word 'commute' for the first time. Bilbao was only 25 kilometres away, and little caravans of smart cars would soon be honking the oxen off the narrow roads in the early hours of the morning.

Senor Etxebeste knew a market when he saw one - a gift he was to pass on, though he must have bitterly regretted it, to Jon. He sold off two parcels of his land at the edge of the town to the developers, knocked down the nameless part-time bar where he used to serve half a dozen neighbours in the evening, more for company than cash, and built the Ama Lur. That's the Basque for Mother Earth - the rising generation of young Basque nationalists were dipping into the cosmopolitan fleshpots as Franco's archaic moral and economic restrictions collapsed, but they liked to keep faith with the rural pieties of their forefathers. The world was changing, and Senor Etxebeste thought he knew how to change with it, though he had no idea how fast or far-reaching the changes would be. He thought he knew when to go forward and when to move back; yes indeed, he believed he knew his market.

So it did annoy him to see Jon's sloppy *cuadrilla*, several of whom were children of the outsiders, lounging against his stainless steel bar five times a day. It annoyed him especially when the elegant young couples from Bilbao paused at his panoramic plate-glass window, and passed on to the old bar across the street, where they didn't even serve draft beer, but where some of the authentic atmosphere of the old Basque countryside seemed to be preserved. Still, his son's labour came a lot cheaper than the going rate, and at least Jon didn't have his hand in the till, so he probably reckoned that things balanced out, at least in the beginning. And if Jon chaffed to have his freedom, his privileged position behind the bar had its advantages. One of the girls, and not necessarily the same one either, always offered to help clean tables and wipe the bar when the long day was over, and discretion as well as shutters came down over the windows.

I OBSERVED a lot, you may say. Well, there wasn't much else to do in the long lunch hours, or the longer hours after dinner. I was teaching English to a group of technicians and office workers in the only local factory, a place which exported duck liver paté to the best restaurants all over Spain. The factory worked through the night, and every morning the big trucks rolled down the little road out of the village at 4.00 am, so that their precious cargo would arrive fresh on the tables in Barcelona, Madrid or Granada before nightfall. Sometimes a group of my pupils, who were all men, would come into the Ama Lur, after work, or indeed before the shift began. Sooner or later they would all express their appreciation, lewdly or subtly, according to their style, for the Etxebeste's second child.

I did mention another child, didn't I? Jon's sister - I never learned her name - was perhaps a year younger than he was, and clearly going to be beautiful. Her half-formed figure was already willowy and graceful. She had long, light-brown hair which seemed yellow in certain lights, through which she sometimes threaded a few tight braids. She had liquid, soulful brown eyes, which I think observed much more than mine did. She stayed outside the cosy circle of the *cuadrilla*. Perhaps she kept apart to save Jon the embarrassing presence of a younger sister, but I think her aloofness was also part of her nature.

Whenever she had served anybody, she would gracefully withdraw from the bar immediately, and busy herself with some activity around the coffee machine, or in the deep recesses behind the bar where sandwiches and *pinchos* were prepared. It seemed she could always find a shadow, a distance from the noisy world beyond the counter, from where she could watch without being watched. There was a sadness about her, an awareness, perhaps, that she was going to be so beautiful that men would never love her for herself alone. Maybe that's why she chose the hard path she took in the years that followed.

It always seemed to me that it was their mother who bound these three individuals together into a family, bound them with love. She glowed with quiet, buttery warmth . Whenever she emerged from the family home, which led directly into the bar, the lines on her husband's face would ease, Jon would bask visibly in the full warmth of her affection, and her daughter would permit herself a half-smile that looked happy enough. Senora Etxebeste's radiance was all-embracing, like sunlight, but it could burn sharply as well.

Simply by calling his name, she could chivvy Jon into washing glasses he had neglected under his father's weary eyes. Without a word spoken, she could bustle her increasingly listless husband into bringing in the crates of soft drinks which otherwise often stood for hours where the delivery man had left them, outside the door. It was harder to see what effect she had on her daughter. The girl's inner authority was already such that she seemed to need no direction from outside herself, and the recesses for which she was responsible were, in any case, always as orderly as her mother could possibly desire. Now that I think of it, Senora Etxebeste didn't serve much in the bar that year, because there was a young child upstairs.

ONE Saturday evening, later in that year of riots and referenda, I found myself wandering through the old quarter of Bilbao, the Siete Calles, whose famous bars always disappointed me. Mostly tacky and obscurely sordid, they were barely acceptable as refuges from the Dickensian industrial wasteland which stretched for miles along the River Nervion — or from the police. That evening, the air was still acrid from the afternoon's tear gas, and I felt the uneasy churning in my gut which always threatened to betray me when I encountered street fighting. Suddenly, I saw a grey jeep full of riot police (ironically appropriate phrase, that) speed down a narrow road in my direction. With as much haste as was decently possible, perhaps more, I stepped into the nearest bar, gently closing the door behind me. I had seen what these fuckers in their grey uniforms could do when their blood was up, and I also knew that a foreign passport and a foreign accent were no protection at all. Indeed, the more ideologically committed among them — who

115

formed extralegal hit squads with titles like 'The Warriors of Christ the King' - might even see such a passport as a provocation, a sign of the European decadence that threatened their holy remnant of the Spanish empire.

So I didn't pay much attention to the clients of the bar when I entered. I concentrated on getting a half-finished drink in front of me and an impassive impression on my face. The first jeep had already passed, and its inevitable sister could be heard approaching, when my eyes began to grow accustomed to the gloom after the hard June light outside. Even so it was the smell that I noticed first, an unmistakeable whiff of hashish that suddenly interrupted the usual olfactory battle between the garlic from the kitchen, the coffee and cigars from the bar, and the residue of teargas from the street.

I couldn't help glancing around, and saw a familiar-looking youth hunched over a table with one of the barmen, discussing something seriously in low voices. I began to feel other eyes on me, and, for once, was glad of my foreign accent as I ordered a second drink. I might be an outsider, but that made me all the less likely to be any threat to the business in hand here. Just as I finished the drink, Jon rose from the table and, with only a slight hesitation to betray his recognition, walked past me and out into the street. What struck me most was not that he had not greeted me, but that, for the first time I could remember, there was no trace of a smile on his hard, nervous face.

We never acknowledged that encounter during the few weeks that were left to me in the village, but I felt him glance sideways at me whenever I entered the bar. I also felt, though it may have been imagination, that there was an all-too-familiar lassitude among the members of the *cuadrilla*, and a sense that they were now bound against the world not just by the awkward exuberance of youth, but by a common secret. And when she moved out of the shadows at all, Jon's sister's eyes took on a sharper, more guarded tone.

The rest is mainly snapshots. Over the next ten years I returned to the village irregularly, five or six times, and sometimes only stayed for a few hours. Usually, though, I would drop in to have a drink at the Ama Lur. Some visits have now blurred into others, but I distinctly remember the great warmth with which Jon greeted me the first time I went back, as though we had been old friends. I cannot recall that we had ever exchanged more than perfunctory, albeit amicable, phrases in all the months I had lived there, but now he was suddenly chattering animatedly about every topic under the sun. I told him that I had become a journalist, and he mentioned that his sister was now living "on the other side", that she was in touch with exiles like Txomin Garaikoetxea, and that I might like to use her as a contact, though he added at once that he thought all that political stuff was shit, personally. Before I could get her number from him, two kids from the *cuadrilla* came in, with two more I didn't recognise. Jon abruptly excused himself, leaving the bar unattended to take them into a quiet corner of the lounge. When I went to the toilets, I noticed that there was no soap in the dispensers.

THREE years later, perhaps, I was back again, and called into the bar late at night. It was full of noisy young people, none of them very smartly dressed. Senor Etxebeste served me, gesturing half apologetically at the nervous and somehow unhappy bustle that stretched from the bar to the plate glass windows. The muzak was almost unbearably loud, Basque punk bands hissing out atonal phrases in a new urban dialect not even Xabier could have translated. Senora Etxebeste came in, visibly bristled at the mess that littered the bar and the tables, and, marching through the clients as though they were soldiers from an occupying army, gathered glasses - mainly empty- onto a tray. She shouted to Jon, who was somewhere in the thick of things, to help her. He smiled charmingly, made a helpless gesture, and ignored her request. She looked so terribly hurt that, for a brief moment, I was horribly certain that she was going to cry.

Then she stiffened her back and clattered out past us. Senor Etxebeste busied himself at the coffee machine.

As I left, I noticed a new graffito spray painted on the wall opposite: *"Camelos al paredon - Jarrai"*. Death to camels, I thought to myself, what the fuck does that mean? Perhaps 'camel' was a new euphemism for informer. *Jarrai* was a youth branch of ETA, and their threats were no joke. A struggling freelance photographer, whose real crime had been to join the Madrid-based Socialist Party in a nearby village dominated by Basque separatists, had been shot the week before, and I had covered his funeral.

Camels, I ascertained from colleagues the next day, were drug traffickers. ETA supporters, losing ground in an increasingly confident Spanish democracy, had launched a vigorous campaign against the vast influx of heroin into the Basque Country. The police, they said, were actually encouraging drug abuse to divert the next generation of Basque youth from supporting the national liberation struggle. There certainly were some guardias cynical enough to think that they slept safer in their beds if the local kids carried syringes in preference to Parabellums. But the drugs would have got in anyway, as they did everywhere else, even if some border guards hadn't turned a blind eye. The result, in any case, was that drug pushers joined the long list of ETA's "legitimate targets".

THAT campaign was still in full swing when I returned a few months later. I remember attending a *verbena*, that part of a fiesta where a huge bonfire is lit in the village square. After some artless but exuberant street theatre, in which local children played witches and goblins, there was a sudden silence. Four youths masked in balaclavas, one of them a girl with long yellow hair which poured down out of her mask, emerged from a side street. They were carrying, coffin-fashion, a giant syringe made of polystyrene, which they ceremonially threw on the fire to scattered applause, as an anti-drug chant rose from two or three sections of the crowd. It was quickly drowned by the thick black smoke which belched from the burning plastic, and drove the choking revellers from the square.

Slightly sickened by the fumes, I called up to the Ama Lur for a restorative brandy. It was almost empty, but then the rapid ebb and flow of customers, even or especially during fiestas, is part of the Basque drinking tradition, which demands that you move rapidly from bar to bar. Jon's vastly extended *cuadrilla*, however, had seemed to be poor respecters of this tradition, and I was surprised to see him alone behind the bar, without a customer to talk to. As I came closer, I saw that his leg was in plaster and he had a crutch beside him.

"What happened you", I asked genially but stupidly, "you make some woman too excited?"

He glared at me first, then gripped me fiercely by the elbow. His father, who had been fiddling with the coffee machine, slipped out of earshot.

"Listen, journalist," said Jon, "maybe you'd like to write about this. Some of your political friends came in here last month with two pistols and one power drill. They forced me up on the bar and made me take my trousers off. Then my underpants. They pointed one pistol at my head, the other at my balls. It was late but the bar was still half-full. Of my friends, you understand? It got very quiet, but they left the music on. Los Rolling Stones, if you want to know. They didn't say a word. They plugged in the drill behind the coffee machine and, taking their time you understand, they drilled into my kneecap. I don't know how, but I didn't let a sound escape. When they left, half the bar started screaming. Then I was flailing around on the bar, crying and shaking. I collapsed into the sink and don't remember anything else.

"I swear I never sold anything but hashish, except maybe a little acid to friends. These people are worse than the police, and I can only talk about it to foreigners. What's happening here?"

As he was finishing, his mother came out. She came over and stood right beside him.

"This is how we are now," she said simply. "Are you enjoying your holiday?"

"He's working here now, Mama," said Jon, "as a journalist."

"Promise me one thing", she said, taking my hand. I've never forgotten the warmth and urgency of her grasp. "I never really spoke to you, but you always seemed a nice man. Write nothing about this. Things are bad enough as they are."

THE next time I saw her was last night. I knew what had happened since we had spoken, but somehow I had to go into the bar. Maybe I wanted to try to commiserate with her but, as I said, she didn't seem to recognise me, and I couldn't bring myself to remind her who I was. Maybe I just went in out of ghastly, irrestible, curiosity.

They had told me in the bar across the road that Jon had continued selling drugs after his knee-capping. He had happened to be out when ETA came for him again. They wrecked the bar and told his parents that he should leave the country if he wanted to stay alive. He had gone into hiding in a hut up the mountains, but they found him there a week later and shot him dead. Only his sister, it was whispered, could have guided them to his hiding place. Did I know that she had become Txomin Garaikoetxea's lover? That Txomin had been found and shot in a safe house by right-wing terrorists who got their information from the police? That ETA said, in the communique in which they announced the 'execution' of Jon Etxebeste, that he had been not only a drug pusher but an informer, who had betrayed the whereabouts of one of their leaders to the police in exchange for a promise of protection? That they had warned all future collaborators to note that no fascist police force could protect them from revolutionary justice?

I don't know how much of this was true, but an agony beyond telling was etched eloquently on Senora Etxebeste's face. Then something happened that turned my own face whiter than my coffee cup. Jon himself entered the bar from the house.

It took me two full takes to realise that it was not Jon but his younger brother, of whom I had been only vaguely aware, and who was now the age Jon had been when I first met him. The nucleus of a *cuadrilla* was waiting for him at the bar. Pride and anxiety fought in his mother's face as she watched him serve them tonics, red wine, and *zurritos*. He chatted to his friends, some of whom had been Jon's friends, with all of his brother's easy, smiling charm. I went to the toilet before I left, and saw that the soap dispensers had been ripped out of the wall, not by ETA, presumably, because the containers still lay on the floor. Beside them was a used syringe, with traces of blood on the needle.

AFTER the concert, though it was very late, I asked Xabier to drive me to the graveyard where Jon was buried. As we approached, a young woman was hurriedly getting into a car where three men were waiting. She had long hair, but I couldn't tell its colour in the darkness. There was no moon, and it took us a while to find Jon's monument. It was simple but had cost money: an ancient solar emblem machine-carved and polished on granite, a rare stone in the Pyrenees. The inscription, in Basque, was also simple: To Jon, to our much-loved and loving son. The funeral wreaths were long-since faded, but an anonymous bunch of hand-picked wild-flowers had been freshly set in a wine-bottle beside the stone.

Later, we went over to look at the clock tower, but we could make out no message whatsoever about the passage and ultimate impact of the striking hours.

THE BABY CARRIAGE

Eugene McEldowney

YOU know, there's often a lot of truth in those old sayings you hear people coming out with from time to time, mostly without thinking. Take for instance that proverb about counting your chickens, and take Joe Carradine, or rather, take his wife, Kitty, for she's a good example of what I'm trying to say.

When I first met Joe, he was a young lad, just like myself, not long out of school and into his first job. In fact it was Kitty persuaded him to take it for I learnt afterwards that he'd been offered a post with the Great Northern Railways at more money, but he turned it down. The way Kitty figured it, there might have been more money with the GNR to start, but the prospects weren't so good. She had her eye fixed on the future, you see, even then, and Joe was so much cracked on her at the time, that he would have done anything she told him.

We were trainee advertising reps and in those days things were very formal and you had to dress the part - three-piece suits and button waistcoats, starch collars and shiny boots. Old Mr Harris, who was the supervisor, was the very divil for tidiness. He used to give us the line that when we were out selling ads we were representing the company and what sort of an impression would we make if we went around dressed like scarecrows. That sort of stuff. And nobody ever argued or questioned. You wouldn't have dared.

The first time I met Kitty was on a Saturday afternoon about six months after I'd joined the firm. I was staying in digs at the time and I just wandered into town for something to do. I bumped into the pair of them near the top of Grafton Street.

She was a pleasant little thing, not what you'd call beautiful, but as bright as a button, and I remember thinking at the time that she had very good style and made the most of what features she had. She was wearing a dark tweed suit and a nice little hat with a veil, that drew attention to her dark looks, and she'd a touch of rouge on her cheeks and just a hint of perfume.

We had afternoon tea in Bewleys and afterwards we went for a stroll and it was clear as anything that Joe thought the world of her. He was as proud as punch to be walking out with her on his arm through Stephen's Green of a Saturday afternoon with half of Dublin looking on. I could see him peeping over at me from time to time to gauge my reaction, trying to catch me unawares and to tell you the truth I was quite impressed, for I'd no girl of my own at the time and it seemed the height of sophistication to be walking out.

And Kitty was good company. She wasn't a bit shy and she'd plenty of conversation. She talked on about the theatre and the drama society and said we'd have to make an outing some night to the Theatre Royal. She said she could arrange tickets.

I used to see them often in the morning, on the way into work. They both lived on the north side, and they'd get the tram together and walk as far as the Ballast Office at the corner of Westmoreland Street. Joe'd give her a little peck on the cheek and off she'd go up along the quays to the solicitors' office where she was working at the time as a secretary. Joe'd stand watching after her till she'd gone a few hundred yards and when she was out of sight he'd walk to the tobacconists and buy himself a packet of cigars with the air of a well-contented man. I didn't know much about these things at the time, but it seemed clear to me they were in love.

Mind you there was no doubting who had the upper hand. In those days the single men in the office used to go over to the Palace Bar in Fleet Street on Friday evenings when we'd finished work and we'd have a few drinks just because it was the weekend. It was harmless enough. Joe'd buy a drink and then I'd buy a drink and if Kinsella was with us, he'd chip in too. And then we'd all say goodnight and off we'd go home about eight o'clock for our supper. No-one ever got drunk, for apart from anything else we hadn't the sort of money to do any heavy tippling. It was just a sort of male ritual thing, letting off a little bit of steam, discussing office politics when the week's work was done. Maybe that's why Kitty intervened. That and the few bob. Joe just announced one Friday afternoon that he wouldn't be going over to the Palace after work. Kitty had said it was a waste of money, and apart from that Harris mightn't approve. "Remember", Joe said, with a sage look, "Paddy Conroy got fired because a client complained that he had drink on his breath when he called for an ad one afternoon."

Well I didn't argue with him, for what he and Kitty decided to do was their own business, but we missed him at the Friday night sessions and I wasn't a bit surprised when he took me aside one lunchtime and told me that they were getting engaged and were going to get married in the summer when he'd finished his training.

Kitty wasn't the sort of girl to watch good money going to keep Guinness's in business when it could be much better spent on a deposit for the little house she was planning out in Fairview. That was Kitty all over. She left nothing to chance. Everything had to be organised. And of course Joe fell in with all her plans.

It was a quiet wedding, just a few family friends and myself and a small bit of a reception afterwards and then the pair of them were off to Tramore for the honeymoon.

They used to invite me out to the new house for Sunday lunch. I think they were a wee bit lonely but it made a break to get away from the digs and besides, Kitty was a great cook, so I used to look forward to it.

It was at one of these lunches that the subject came up about starting a family. Kitty had to stop work, of course, when she got married and it seemed a natural enough topic to raise. I'm not sure whether it was me who brought it up, but it soon became clear that Joe was a bit embarrassed by it all.

"We'll have children," said Kitty ladling out carrots onto my plate, "whenever we've got everything else sorted out. My Goodness, sure we haven't even started to furnish the house properly yet. You're a scream. If you knew what we have to pay back on the mortgage, and then trying to save for furniture on top of that, you wouldn't be going on about babies. Time enough for babies when everything else is good and organised."

"But that's men all over," she said, with that high-pitched little giggle of hers and a flirty glance over to Joe.

I must have been fairly naive at the time, for I remember that the whole business struck me as a bit of a mystery. Either you had children or you didn't. I wasn't aware that you had to plan for them. But rather than seem foolish, I said nothing, just passed the salt cellar over to Kitty and began cutting at the meat, my head down to avoid their eyes.

Well, they must have changed their minds or something for it wasn't long afterwards that Joe came into work one morning with a big grin on his face. He sat down on the edge of my desk before he'd even got his coat off and he leaned over with a conspiratorial air and says: "Guess what? We've done it. Kitty's expecting."

"That's great news," I said. "Kitty must be delighted."

Joe's grin changed to a worried smile and he said: "Well she is and she isn't. I think it took her a bit by surprise. She'd have preferred to wait for a while, you know, till we'd got a bit more on our feet. Babies are fierce expensive items and we're up to here as it is." He made a slicing motion at his throat.

Still, whether the baby was a surprise or not, Kitty soon slotted the reality into her scheme of things and she wasn't long sorting everything out and getting ready for the big event. She went about it with her usual enthusiasm. The first thing I noticed was this enormous baby carriage blocking the hallway, the next time I was out for Sunday lunch. It was an expensive model, with massive big wheels, all the best material and a little parasol to keep the sun off the baby's eyes when it came along. And before long the place was coming down with cots and baby things and Kitty was constantly knitting clothes.

She used to sit in the big armchair beside the fireplace, growing plumper by the week, the knitting needles flashing and Joe fussing around her like a mother hen. Kitty enjoyed every minute of it. She'd spend hours working out names, planning the child's education, shaping its career. Because the baby was due to be born in June, she got the notion that it was going to be musical and nothing would do her but she'd have to get these piano catalogues from McCullough Piggott's in Suffolk Street.

Joe pretended to humour her any time I was there, laughing at all this female extravagance but I could see that beneath it all he was delighted that Kitty was so content. They were so much in love, you see.

True to Type

The child was born dead. A little boy, two months premature. Kitty seemed to take it pretty well. It was Joe who went to pieces.

I left them alone for a while after that, not wanting to intrude on their grief. And maybe I was wrong about that, for a few weeks later I got a letter from Kitty saying that if I didn't come out to see her, she'd personally come into the office and drag me out. So the following Sunday I went to lunch with them, a bit reluctantly it's true, but I knew it had to come sooner or later. As it turned out there was no need for any apprehension. At least not as far as Kitty was concerned. She met me at the door, and took the flowers I'd brought and poured me a bottle of stout, all the time chatting away about everything except the one topic that lay between us. It wasn't until we were sitting at the dining table and the meal was served, that she brought the subject up.

"I just want to tell you," she said, "that as far as we're concerned what's done is over and past and there's nothing anyone can do to alter it. It was God's will and we must accept it. Joe and I have had a long talk with the doctor and he's told us there's no reason why we shouldn't have more children. We've made up our minds that we're not going to brood about it. And we're not going to let any-one else brood about it either. And that goes for you." She hit me a playful rap across the knuckles with her spoon so that I was forced to smile.

"Here, Joe," she said. "Get him another bottle of stout." And Joe just got up from the table and went off into the scullery and came back with a bottle for each of us and for the remainder of the meal he hardly said two words, leaving all the small talk up to Kitty. Af-ter that day, the subject was never raised again, but it seemed to me that Joe had lost the cheerful spark he used to have. He got more and more withdrawn, hardly talking to anyone in the office, and although I still went out to see them, it got to be more of a duty.

And always that big baby carriage stood solid in the hallway, shining new like the day it was bought, so that in time it came to represent a sort of symbol of defiance as much as anything else. When it finally went I knew a crisis had arrived, although I didn't know then what sort. The official reason for selling the carriage was that they needed the money. As usual, it was Kitty who broke the news. "We decided to get rid of it," she said in an off-hand way.

"to raise a little bit of spare cash. Joe's going to decorate the parlour over the Easter, and you know how tight things are with money, specially since Harris cut back on the overtime. And anyway we're fed up looking at it to tell you the truth. It's been there for over a year, for God's sake." And she added a little throw-away remark aimed more at Joe, I thought, than me. "Sure whenever we need another one, we can easily go out and get it."

Well after that, things seemed to go down hill at an alarming rate. Joe took up the Friday night drinking sessions again. Indeed he quickly became the mainstay of the occasions, encouraging the rest of us to stay on long after we would normally have gone home. And it was at one of these sessions that I learnt they had split up. Nothing would do Joe but we'd all get a cab out to Fairview. When I remarked that Kitty would be delighted to have a posse of drunkards arrive on her doorstep, he stopped short and waved an unsteady finger at me, and said she'd gone to stay with her mother for a while. He didn't make up any excuses for Kitty's departure and he didn't mention it again and neither did I, but I turned down his invitation to go out to the house.

They got together again. I think some priest friend of his mother's intervened, but it didn't last and in a matter of months, they were separated once more. And then, the next thing I heard, they were in the process of selling the house so I knew it was serious. I was very embarrassed about the whole business, for that sort of thing wasn't very usual. And being a friend to both of them, I felt that maybe I should get involved and try and patch things up. But I didn't know what to do, so in the end I took the coward's way out and did nothing. And that was probably the best thing.

Joe pulled himself together after a while and stopped drinking and before long, I discovered that he was walking out with another young lady who worked in the Bank of Ireland at College Green. I don't know if he told her that he was already married, but if he did, she didn't seem to mind. In fact I ran into them a couple of times around the town and once he even introduced us. Rose, I remember her name was. They seemed happy enough.

I didn't see Kitty for a long time, and when I did she hadn't changed one bit. She was still the same bouncy little ball of energy. She seemed determined to get on with her life and not let things get her down. It was in O'Connell Street one lunchtime, and she just grabbed my arm and wheeled me into the nearest cafe and we sat down by the window and ordered tea and buns. "And how is life treating you?" she said, sipping at her tea. "Oh, so so," I replied. I was a bit nervous at the encounter. "Ah, but you always had good sense," she said. "Enough sense at any rate, not to get married."

"It wasn't a conscious decision. Just that I haven't met the right woman yet." She smiled at the banality of the remark and I thought for a second that she was making fun of me. But then she adopted a serious tone and rapped me on the knuckles with her tea-spoon. Suddenly I remembered the last time she had done that. "When you do meet the right woman," she said, "just make sure that she is the right woman. And don't go rushing things. Take your time and get to know her well before you make any big decisions. It's amazing what you discover about people once you live with them." I took her hand and pressed it. "I'm sorry about the whole business. I really am." But Kitty just shook her hair back and laughed. "Oh that's all water under the bridge," she said. "I've put it down to experience." "I suppose it was the baby?" She paused for a moment before replying. "Yes, it probably was. At least that's what started it. When the child was born dead it was an awful blow to Joe. He took it personally, as if it was his fault. Then nothing would do him but we'd have another one, and when that didn't happen it only made matters worse. Joe was very immature, you know." I noticed that she said was, as if Joe was dead.

We finished our tea and I left her to the door and waved her on her way up O'Connell Street, watching her bobbing in and out of the crowds and sure enough when she'd gone a few hundred yards she turned back and waved again. I walked back to the office feeling pretty big for my boots and thinking what a fool Joe had been to have lost Kitty and let his marriage break up over a dead child. It was only years later that I came to realise that it wasn't the baby at all. It was Kitty and her failure to control things. The miscarriage and all that business only brought it home to Joe that Kitty had feet of clay, just like the rest of us. And he couldn't live with that. That's what really caused it.

FORGET THE FRONT PAGE

Tom Glennon

IT was a nice, balanced front page and those damned Turks had to screw it all up. Frank looked away wearily from the news despatches piling up in front of him and thought: "Paper, paper everywhere and not a drop to drink."

He had had a few drinks across the road and had put the paper safely to bed when the Turks at an unearthly hour of the morning had invaded Cyprus. "Why couldn't they pick another morning, another time?

"What a way to earn a crust? Just when you thought you had a soft night, some lunatic does something even more lunatic. Cypriots and Turks, Christians and Saracens. How far did it all go back? To the Crusades? Even further. Would they ever learn?

"The Romans knew how to deal with them all, Cypriots or Turks. Crush the bastards!"

He looked over at his assistant, Sam, concentrating on sorting the despatches about the invasion. "They knew how to deal with the Christians too," Frank thought.

He went down to the print section and changed the front page again. Take another story inside, shift that picture, throw that out altogether. With a war on, nobody's going to miss an illiterate speech mouthing nothings by an illiterate politician. You had to be ruthless in this game.

He sent the front page again for printing, then back at his desk upstairs another pile of despatches lay in front of him. From all the news agencies – analysis, conjecture, pure fiction, churned out at this unearthly hour by old sweats like himself half suffering from a hangover. Hard graft and stamina.

"We'll replate the front page again in twenty minutes," he said.

There was an air of tension, even for a newspaper office, about the place. People were treading around as if there were eggs on the floor. Wars didn't break out every day.

He thought of the Cypriots mowing down the invading Turks and the Turks mowing down the defending Cypriots. Ships, tanks, planes, landing-craft, guns, casualties, maiming, cripples, weeping widows and mothers – men loved war, they loved swimming in blood, he thought. Blood, bandages, glory.

He looked out at the first faint glimmer of the summer dawn. The seagulls were on the windowsills looking for scraps. "Somebody feed the seagulls," he shouted to the copy-boy. "They didn't start this blasted war."

Sam and the copy-boy were whispering together. All civilised people except Turks and Cypriots, seagulls and newspapermen were in bed, Frank thought. All this toil for a glance from a reader at the front page before he burrows into the paper for his real interest, the racing page.

Sam came over hesitantly with another despatch in his hand.

"What's that?" Frank demanded.

"It's from Milwaukee," said Sam.

"Milwaukee? I didn't know there were Turks in Milwaukee. The only thing they know about Turkey in Milwaukee is what they see on a plate on Thanksgiving Day."

Sam muttered: "It's nothing to do with the war."

Frank read it: "A reporter, Emily Dawson, with the *Milwaukee Courier* this morning gave birth to a baby boy in the newsroom. Foreign papers please copy."

"What joker sent this?" he demanded. "What am I supposed to do? Send them gold, frankincense and myrrh? Offer to be the godfather?"

"We could send a reply," said Sam. "It's not often women reporters have babies in newsrooms."

"Women having babies during wars and invasions. Procreation and war go hand in hand," Frank murmured to a vague tune. "Will they ever learn? They're just producing more cannon fodder for the next War to End All Wars."

The despatch from Milwaukee lay on his desk as he rushed to prepare for the next replating of the front page.

"Bring that down and get it set pronto," he shouted at the copyboy.

Sam came over again: "Forget the front page for a minute, Frank. Are you going to do anything about that?"

"About what?"

"That despatch from Milwaukee about the baby. We could send a message of congratulations," Sam stammered.

He looked at Sam, puzzled. "I'm dealing with an invasion and a war. This is not a cards for all occasions boutique, you know." Then he softened a bit: "You send a reply if you want to, but warn the woman to keep the boy away from newspapers. Tell her to make him into something respectable like a whorehouse manager or running a crocodile farm."

Sam went into the despatch room to send the already prepared message to Milwaukee. Frank rushed downstairs to replate the front page for the last time.

Half-an-hour later, he relaxed smoking at his desk. "That's all we can do, Sam," he said. "The evenings can pick it up from here. Come on, we'll just get in across the road for a few before they close up. We can drink to maimed Turks and Cypriots and to that baby in Milwaukee."

Sam dropped another despatch from Milwaukee in front of Frank. It read: "Congratulations Dublin. First foreign reaction. Mother and baby (8 lbs) doing well. Will call him Patrick."

Frank read it and read it again. For the first time that day he showed a tinge of emotion. "Another Paddy to either populate the world or go out to convert the heathen," he muttered to no-one in particular as he got up to go.

IN PROSPERITY AND ADVERSITY

Pat Comerford

IT must have been Peter, while we were still children, who first took to calling him the White Rabbit. Once given, the name stuck. That afternoon, Canon Phillips looked every bit the White Rabbit: his thin, white hair fell limply around his pink face; his pink, shell-rimmed glasses failed to disguise his blood-shot, weak eyes; a full, long and starched white surplice almost totally covered his cassock, and a broad creamy, white stole had been donned especially for Peter's wedding.

The White Rabbit stood before us, squat, rigid, and drumming his right fingers on the Prayer Book he was keeping open in his left palm, occasionally muttering the opening sentences of the service, "Dearly beloved, we are gathered...", as if rehearsing the wedding to himself, or testing to see if he could remember all the words.

"I understand the propriety of a bride wanting to be late," he intoned, impatient that he had to interrupt himself. "Five minutes, ten at the most. But" – and he hissed as he looked up at the clock at the west end of the church – "sixteen minutes seems extravagant." Nervously, I nudged Peter; there might have been a knowing grin in his facial reply, except he was still anxious and upset.

It all came to a climax the previous evening. As Peter's best man, I had put a lot of thought into planning the stag night he wanted. He never took to Dublin stags in sleezey, smokey pubs that ended in disreputable night-clubs, and so he had planned for weeks to come home with my brother Rick in time for a proper night on the old town.

The Bohemian Girl... the bar in White's... The Eagle Bar... Con Macken's and The Cape... Jack Fane's and Tommy Roche's...

Rick wanted to prove there were more pubs on the Quay side of Main Street, "so they could roll the barrels off the ships straight into the basements". But by the time we reached the Tower Bar in our pilgrimage through the pubs of the Bull Ring and the Main Street, Rick was too drunk to restate the finer points of his history lesson, and I was sure Peter was drawn and pale only because he had five too many. It wasn't much to worry about, we had all experienced similar feelings in the rugby club on many of our more youthful weekends.

But just as I thought it was time to move on to the Commodore, Peter was missing. I slipped quietly from the bar, which Rick was grabbing solidly with his left hand as he held a fresh pint up to his mouth with his right. "Tell us, John, is it true you spent your snag tight...?" He started to reminisce, but wasn't even finishing his questions, and I thought Peter must be feeling sick if he had to spend that much time away from the two of us. I headed for the basement, wondering whether he had gone down to the men's loo, but as I opened the bar door into the side hallway I could hear his quiet, sober, worried voice on the phone at the lounge door.

"Yes June, thanks... No, I understand... Please... don't...I'm sorry, I am sorry." Then he caught me in the corner of his eye. "I must go now, June, thanks...Yes, I do...I really am sorry." But there was no "See you later," no "I love you".

Quietly, he hung up the phone, turned to me and pleaded: "John, I don't feel like going on". But he didn't look into my face as he begged, almost sobbed: "Can we go back to your place? I'm not on for any more drinking."

I poked my head back around the bar door: "Rick, follow us back up to my place, will you? John and I are going on ahead."

Rick still had more than half a pint in his hand; I could take Peter away and find out what was troubling him before Rick realised it. As we headed out the side door and began to make our way up Rowe Street, Peter still looked pale. "There's no point in going back to my place if you're feeling like that. Do you want some fresh air along the Quays? And you can tell me what's bothering you."

We doubled back silently, passed on down Church Lane between St Iberius and the Foresters' Hall, and down the side of the car park. Peter said nothing as we crossed over the road onto the wooden-works and the trainline and began to make our way down the Quays. It was still bright, and orange streaks were beginning to break through the evening clouds over the harbour. The only sounds as we walked along Commercial Quay and Custom House Quay were a few passing cars, the birds hovering on the harbour water, and a handful of children playing around the ropes of the Guillemot moored against the Quay wall.

We reached the Crescent before I started to ask any questions: "Well Pete, what's the problem? Has June got butterflies? Is she having second thoughts?"

"Well, no, not exactly."

"Not exactly? So there is a problem?"

"Well, of sorts. Look, you'll stand beside me tomorrow, John, won't you."

"What do you think I am?" I asked. "Is there some problem between you and June? Do you want me to run you over to her place in the car?"

"No, no don't, please."

"It'll only take ten or fifteen minutes."

"No," he insisted.

By now we were facing each other in the car park beside the gasworks in Trinity Street, opposite the Talbot, and I still hadn't rumbled what was wrong. "Look Peter, if you and June have some problem, you'd better sort it out now. Because, tomorrow is going to be too late."

I wasn't prepared for what he said next: "John, we have talked it out. We're not getting married." He looked away from me and out towards the Ballast Bank and the breakwater. "Not tomorrow, not ever."

I PEERED down at the mud in the Crescent as Peter told me a story I had never prepared myself to hear. On the way down from Dublin with Rick, it had dawned on him slowly that although he and June were the best of friends, "I just couldn't honestly say I was in love. I had to face up to that before it was too late."

With arms swinging slowly, limply over the rusty rails, he went on to explain his absence once we had arrived in the Tower Bar. "By then, I had plucked up enough courage to ring her and explain that although I liked her a lot, that I would always see her as a really close friend, my special friend, I knew I wasn't ready to go ahead with getting married, not now and not with her."

I wanted to ask him if he was just suffering from pre-marital jitters, but he continued to talk without any prompting.

"I told her I was sorry, and that I couldn't think of how to apologise. And you know what? She just told me she understood. She promised we'd stay friends, and said she'd look after explaining everything to her family later on. That, and sending back our wedding presents as well."

"What then?"

"Oh, we'll meet back in Dublin next week and sort all that out — what to do about the deposit and the builders, keeping on the flat, and all those things. She just asked me for one favour before then."

"And what's that?" I asked, torn between my cynicism, my anger, my feelings about how lost and lonely June must have been that evening, and my loyalty to Peter.

"She wanted to know would we keep it quiet, and just turn up in Church tomorrow afternoon."

"She what?" I didn't understand. "What do you mean?"

"Well, she pointed out that if we started trying to call off the wedding now, at this time of the night, everyone would panic, and she'd have to explain to her mother that I'd called it off. There'd be a row, and we'd have to wait months before sorting things out with the bank and the house. And she'd always have the reputation of having been jilted."

That was typical of Peter – practical down to the last detail, whatever the emotional feelings. I felt more sorry for June than for Peter, even if he is my cousin.

"Well," I suggested with resigned but sorry feelings, "I suppose it's much easier for a man to say he was left at the altar because she had bad nerves, than it is for someone like June to live with the name of being a jilted woman."

"Exactly, that's just how June put it. She said we could just turn up at St Machta's, pretend nothing's happened, and when the car arrived at her house she'd tell her mother she couldn't go through with it, pretend she'd been having second thoughts for a long time, that sort of thing."

I thought Peter was being a coward, leaving all that for June to carry with her for the next eighteen hours, but all I could blurt out was: "The White Rabbit will be ripping mad".

"I know. June said he'd told her she could be late, five minutes late, but no more. She says when it comes to twenty past, you can tell Canon Phillips she musn't be coming. She knows his bad temper will be enough to let him believe the whole thing should be called off."

Now he had put an extra burden on me too. But soon I was thinking: "Poor Peter". I hadn't realised what he'd been going through. But from the way he told it, sounded as if June had been a far more understanding friend than either Rick or I had been to him since we were children.

"Let's get back to the Tower Bar and collect Rick," I said. And Peter made a last request: "Not a word to Rick either, please."

When we found Rick, he was deep in conversation about election promises, the trade union movement and the coalition. None of it made sense and he hardly even noticed we'd been gone for 40 minutes. "I want to go on to the Commodore," he protested. "I won't finish drinking until we reach the Stone Bridge. Or even better, the Tablet Hotel." He was triumphant, but he left calmly and mildly when we insisted it was time to go. It was dark as all three of us finally headed up Rowe Street and back to my place.

HAVING crossed the front of the church and crossed it again at least four times in as many minutes, Canon Phillips was back in front of us again. This time his impatience had turned to anger, and his face was flushed with rage.

"Well, does the groom have anything to say for himself or his bride? It's now getting after twenty past and I can't see why I should be left here standing all afternoon. I'm a retired man now, you know. I'm only doing this as a special favour for your family. Has the best man anything to say in your defence?"

I looked at Peter, who was beginning to relax. I could see relief in his eyes as he began to accept that June was not turning up. What a friend he had in her. Few men have wives who are friends like that, I thought, as I looked at the White Rabbit and began to speak up for Peter.

"Er, eh, Canon Phillips, I think I should..."

"Should nothing my man," he quipped back, looking straight down the nave. Rick still had a hangover and noticed nothing, but Peter and I were stunned as we turned our heads in disbelief. There, hand looped through her brother's arm, steadily making her way up through the pews, was June.

Before we could even turn back and catch each other's eye, the organist was playing, and Canon Phillips assumed a glad voice and feigned informality as he started to intone from his Prayer Book: "Dearly beloved, we are gathered together here in the sight of God, and in the face of this Congregation, to join together this Man, Peter, and this Woman, June, in holy..."

THE GREAT TREK OF WILLEM LOURENS

Seamus Martin

THE small boy cried at the most solemn moment of the Great Rally of the Volk; his sobs ruffled the stillness of the night air just as 20,000 Afrikaaners had fallen into silence at the end of the national anthem, Die Stem van Suid Afrika.

Willem's hair was closely cropped and of that flaxen fairness rarely seen outside northern Europe. His skin was light and soft; the dry heat of the high veld had yet to take its toll. The boy's large ears stood out at perfect right-angles to his head, his white elbows stuck through holes in his tattered school jumper. A high water mark was visible where he had carelessly washed his neck. He wore no shoes and though his thinness stopped short of emacia-tion, it was enough to conjure up pictures of those sunken-eyed Boer boys who had died in their thousands in the first concentra-tion camps the world had known, in the course of the Anglo-Boer war.

Willem Lourens was nine. His trip into Pretoria had been de-cided on only that morning when his father, at breakfast, had read a news item in the African paper he had brought home after he had finished work the night before.

Willem's father was a security guard on the railways and, walk-ing through the carriages, his final shift completed, he checked that nothing sinister had been left behind on the train. Then, on an im-pulse, he did something he had never done before. In the carriages reserved for blacks, someone had left a copy of *City Press* on a seat. Mr Lourens picked it up out of curiosity to read what the black people's paper was printing about the release of more prisoners and the return of more ANC exiles earlier that week. It was a sign that the changing times were having their own effect on his mind, for in the past the thoughts of the blacks, the words of their newspapers, he had not considered worthy of his attention.

Next morning over coffee, having read the triumphant accounts of the welcomings in the townships, he turned to other pages. Across the bottom of page seven a news item stood out. The Transvaal railways would, the report said, have their first black engine drivers in 1995. The significance of this news stuck Hendrik Lourens immediately and with great force; this was something of far greater and more immediate importance than the release of the prisoners or the return of the exiles.

Here was concrete proof that the Volk was being betrayed. Up to now Hendrik had trusted the National Party as he had all his life. He had regarded De Klerk's freeing of Mandela and the others as a gesture to the foreign governments who had imposed sanctions. These acts, he felt, were something of a ruse. The Party would not let its people down.

But this was real trouble. His own, his family's livelihood was now in danger. Jobs previously reserved for whites would now go to blacks.

The decision was taken, there and then, to go the Great Rally of the Volk in Pretoria that afternoon. He would bring Willem, his only son, with him to show the youngster that the blacks were threatening his future, and how the anger of the volk had been roused.

Willem had played and fought and fallen on his journey home from school but despite his mother's pleas that she should be allowed clean him up for the occasion, his father took him directly from the working-class white suburb to the great rally without allowing him enter the house.

"But he'll be hungry" his mother cried.

"The farmers will be there, they will have food" the father replied, and he was right.

By 4.30 the first buses from the Platteland were disgorging their cargoes of outsized countrymen.

There was a picnic atmosphere to begin with in Church Square's pleasant sunken park, edged with jacaranda trees. Neighbours greeted each other warmly, as might be expected in a land where neighbours live scores of miles apart.

The swallows of the African summer swooped over the square in readiness for their great migration to the breeding grounds of Northern Europe; the same swallows perhaps, that swoop in the Irish summer, over the field in Finaghy outside Belfast or the little graveyard at Bodenstown in County Kildare

Old men whittled away at sticks of biltong, the dried meat which sustained their ancestors on the Great Trek. A group of potato farmers, from Bethlehem in the Free State, gathered round the embers of a braaivleis laden with Boer-sausage, steaks and chops, a diet which, over the generations, had turned them into giants.

The heavy afternoon showers of the wet season had died for the day. The sun shone and the talk was of crops and of Platteland gossip; the difficulties of keeping young people on the land and away from the attractions of the devil's city of Johannesburg.

As the Volk gathered, Willem's father had met a group of relatives from Pietersburg in the north. Willem had winced in the embrace of Tant Rika a great smelly hippo of a woman with an uncomfortable and unfeminine growth of beard which had always made him feel uneasy.

She was married to Oom Piet, the small-town cousin of Willem's father, and they had brought their large brood of small children with them.

Tant Rika, told Willem's father of her decision to come to the rally. She had been reading the diaries of Anna Steenkamp, the Voortrekker heroine, niece of the great leader Piet Retief.

"What has changed since Anna Steenkamp's time?" She asked. Hendrik ventured that the Volk had made great advances under their own government but she would have nothing of it. Instead she answered her own question. "Nothing has changed. The blacks were being freed 150 years ago. They are being freed today. Back then our people had their own answer" she said.

Then she opened her copy of the diaries and intoned a passage in her ecclesiastical voice, perfected from listening to sermons every Sunday of her life.

"It is not so much their freedom that drove us to such lengths, as their being placed on an equal footing with Christians, contrary to the laws of God and the natural distinction of race and religion, so that it was intolerable for any decent Christian to bow down beneath such a yoke: wherefore we rather withdrew, thus to preserve our doctrines in purity."

"What was right for our ancestors is right for us", she told Willem's father.

Oom Piet nodded in agreement as he always did when Tant Rika reached back into her Voortrekker past.

Hendrik agreed too and all the while a similar process was going on among the children, at their own level of understanding.

"There were no Kaffirs in South Africa when our people arrived from Holland" said young Carel, adding that he knew this because Meneer Potgieter had said so in school.

"And they want to take our land now" said Elma, another of the Pietersburg tribe.

The boys resented the girl's intervention and switched the talk to Rugby and its Afrikaaner heroes of the Springboks.

"The British and the French and the New Zealanders, they all refuse to play us because they know we will beat them" said Roelof, the cousin nearest Willem's age.

"The others are afraid because we are the best in the world.

That's why they side with the Kaffirs" said Willem who knew this because he had heard his father and his friends say it.

This talk engendered a mock rugby game among the youngsters, a great chase towards an imaginary try-line. Other boys in the gathering crowd joined in. Older men in stiff, dark country suits shouted encouragement, jokingly calling the names of their own rugby heroes: Frik du Preez, Avril Malan, Dawie de Villiers, Naas Botha.

The goal the boys pictured in their minds, stood near a broad flight of steps where a rostrum had been set up and the crowd was thicker. The boys had seen the mass of people at the steps as the crowd in the stands at the Loftus Versfeld, the great stadium of Pretoria and temple of Afrikaner manhood.

Willem was close to the steps when he tired of the game and his attention was drawn to the songs and the hymns and the speeches that had just begun.

A band struck up a hymn to the air of Deutschland Uber Alles and followed it with the sentimental patriotic song Boereplaas which is sung to the air of The Red Flag.

Then Ferdinand Bezuidenhout, a leader of the KP, the Conservative Party, took the microphone. He pointed to the statue of John Paul Kruger which dominated the sunken park.

"There, is a man who would understand the feelings of the Volk; a man who would not surrender to the Afrikaner's enemies" he proclaimed, and the crowd murmured in agreement.

"De Klerk and the traitors are preparing to sell the people's birthright. The Volk should remember its past" he told his followers

"Under Kruger, our good and god-fearing leader, we brought the great British Empire to its knees.

"Under Andries Pretorius a handful of Voortrekkers defeated 10,000 mighty Zulus at the battle of Blood River on the glorious day of December 16th, 1838".

The crowd felt comfortable when they heard these words which they knew so well. Willem knew them too, from school and from his home.

"Tonight the Volk will march from Kruger's Statue in Church Square along the Krugerstraat to Pretorius's statue at the Town Hall. We will show the traitors that the Volk is still strong".

The crowd liked this and so did Willem, for it linked them closer to the heroes of their past and helped them in their own small way to be heroes too.

And at that precise moment an unseen hand, a kilometre away, was placing a flag bearing the Swastika of the Third Reich in the crook of Pretorius's right arm, its staff braced against the bronze hide of his charger.

To the statue's left side, in precisely the same way, was placed the Green, Red, White and Blue Vierkleur of Kruger's old South African Republic.

Willem next saw a local dignitary, Meneer Christiaan Marais, stout, bespectacled and business-suited, like the small-town real-estate agent he was, call for a Dominee of the Dutch Reformed Church to read from the Book of Joel.

The old minister, in a dark brown suit to match his face, turned almost to leather from his long years in the parched climate of the high veld, intoned the message reverently, occasionally being taken with emotion as when he read, from his well-worn bible, the passage: "Gather together the people, sanctify the church, assemble the ancients, gather the little ones and them that suck at the breasts; let the bridegroom go forth from his bed and the bride out of her bride chamber.

"Between the porch and the altar, the priests, the Lord's ministers shall weep and say: 'Spare O Lord, spare thy people and give not thy inheritance to reproach, that the heathen should rule over them. Why should they say among the nations: Where is their God?' "

Willem started as an elderly man, stirred by the rising emotions of the crowd, responded to the Dominee's words in a plaintiff wail like a prophet predicting the apocalypse: "The Hollanders have deserted their own kin; the French and their guns we can trust no more. The Kaffir, the Engelsman and the Communists, surround us".

The boy would see darker things later, after the African night had fallen swiftly. Arms with palms open would shoot in the air at the sight of the Swastika on the statue of Andries Pretorius.

Black youths, straying accidentally on the scene, would be chased down the Schoebertstraat by the big Platteland farmers, with vengeance in their eyes and shouting "Run, Kaffir run".

A man would carry a death-sized carving of a disembodied black head, another an effigy of Mandela on the gallows, yet another would invite the Volk to trample on the Star of David in the flag of Israel.

And later still the man who would be the great leader of the Afrikaner Volk, was to rouse the emotions further. "When the storm comes the eagle soars and the mice run for cover" he would say. And he would inform "Comrade de Klerk" that the Afrikaner Volk was not a nation of mice.

And he too would remind the Volk of the war against the British, of the concentration camps and of the treachery of the black people, of Dingaan who led the noble Piet Retief into his kraal to parley and then killed him

All that was to come soon. But in the here and now, the sad, leather-faced Dominee called on the assembly to stand and sing "Die Stem van Suid Afrika".

Willem had become engrossed in the ritual. A great host of people had built up behind him, the contents of more buses from the Platteland augmented by those, from Pretoria itself, who had joined the rally after they had finished work.

Willem joined the singing in his piping, unbroken voice. He had sung it daily at school assembly, but never with such a feeling of belonging, of being enveloped by his people.

Then the African night fell with its appalling swiftness. It had been daylight when the Dominee chanted the anthem's first words, but now as the final line was sung, the darkness was profound.

So too was the silence. For the vast crowd was struck dumb by the emotions which had poured forth from it. As hands felt for matches to light the torches for the great march, the only sounds to he heard were the sobs of Willem.

But his tears were not for the prophecy that his heritage would be given to reproach, nor that his people would be ruled over by the heathen, nor were they caused by the half-understood worries that the security of his impoverished, god-fearing family would be under threat from the black engine drivers of the future.

He cried for a far more immediate and terrible reason. That feeling of belonging to his people which had engulfed him when the anthem was sung had vanished as quickly as the falling of the night. Here amongst the great mass of the Volk, he realised he was no longer a hero, but just a small boy alone in the dark.

It was an English-speaking woman, a journalist there to cover the rally for the *Johannesburg Star*, who was first to home in on his distress and it was to her, of the stock of the Volk's white enemies that he poured out his grief.

As she tried to comfort him, his shrill, little voice , in his best school-learned English, piped the words: "I HAVE LOST MY PA."

She, whose ancestors had fought and killed the Boers, ushered him up the steps, and handed him back to the Volk.

And the men whose hearts had filled with hatred against their enemies, were now touched with kindness.

The Dominee, who had railed against the heathen, wrapped a

warm hand round the boy. The man with the gallows effigy of Mandela patted him gently on the head.

The great beer-bellied fellow with the Israeli flag, took the boy's little hand and asked his name and where he lived.

Meneer Christiaan Marais went to the microphone and called for "the father of Willem Lourens of Arkadia" to come immediately to the rostrum where his lost son was waiting.

The great march of the Volk from the statue of Kruger to the statue of Pretorius, with the Swastika in the crook of his arm, was delayed for a full five minutes because of the tears of a little boy.

And quickly those tears dried as Willem was once again overcome by the warmth, the protection, the security afforded by the bosom of his people.

The feeling of belonging returned, stronger than before. He was safe in the arms of the Volk; safe from the worries of his family, afe from the threats of strange enemies: the Kaffirs, Mandela, the ommunists, the Jews, the Freemasons, the Engelsman.

he band struck up again.

illem's Great Trek, his march towards the Swastika had begun.

ART, POETRY, MUSIC AND MONEY

Brendan Glacken

THE child was asleep.

Isabel hung her coat carefully on a hanger on the back of the door. She unzipped her sheer skirt, unbuttoned the lace blouse, lay both over a chair and pulled on plain black tracksuit bottoms. Undoing her bra, she laid it carefully with the other clothes and pulled on the tracksuit top, leaving its zip half open.

Reviving the near-dead fire with kindling sticks, and banking it up with the remaining coal, she went into the tiny kitchen, brewed a jug of weak coffee and filled a pitta bread envelope with cottage cheese and sliced tomato. Then, returning to the living-room, she flicked the switch on the large Akai radio-cassette player, sank into the leather armchair and took a sip of coffee.

The Akai was tuned to a slow movement from a symphony which she recognised, but was not immediately able to place. Subdued though the music was, it seemed oddly disquieting. Isabel tried briefly to identify it and then gave up, but could feel the undercurrents of the piece continue to stab her with an almost exquisite pain. On an impulse, she inserted a blank cassette into the Akai and pressed the "record" button. A little red light flickered to life on the machine, fading and glowing as the music ebbed and flowed.

Isabel sank back into the chair, ate her supper slowly, closed her eyes and gave herself over to the seductive harmonies of the music.

The apartment door buzzer sounded. Isabel looked at her small gold watch – it was just after nine o'clock.

"Hi, Isabel. Can I come in?"

It was Douglas Cameron. Isabel felt herself go taut with nervous irritation.

"It's late" she said weakly.

"Late? You weren't always like that, Isabel." Though he refused on what he insisted was principle to wear a watch himself, his quick eye had caught sight of Isabel's pine-and-ceramic wall clock. Isabel, following his eye, then faced him again to find Douglas hungrily taking in the almost completely uncovered expanse of her bosom. Flushing, she zipped up the tracksuit top, turned her back on him and strode into the room.

Closing the door quietly, Douglas followed her. Isabel stood at the table facing him, but with her eyes fixed on the floor and her hands shoved deep in the tracksuit pockets. The young man proceeded to sink himself in the luxurious leather chair, still warm from the woman's body. "Mmmmm" he sighed appreciatively, swivelling the chair slowly through a half-circle: "Always loved this."

He jumped up: "May I?" Without waiting for a response, he slipped out of his heavy, grey herringbone tweed coat, folded the garment casually, tossed it languidly to the corner near the door and sank back again into the yielding leather.

Expressionless, Isabel walked slowly to the door, picked up the coat and arranged it on the hanger along with her own. With her back to Douglas, she fingered the rough tweed of the new coat and passed her hand slowly across the smooth, cold, purple silk lining.

"Oh, you don't need to hang it, Isabel – that thing will look better when it's broken in a bit more. Tweed always does." Douglas's green eyes flickered with amusement. He had glimpsed her caressing the silk: Isabel really was so hopelessly sensual.

"Em – no chance of a cup of coffee, I suppose?"

Isabel glanced at her own unfinished cup, and decided it was not worth while being churlish. "Alright," she said quietly, "But I have to get up in the morning. I don't want to be kept up half the night."

"I understand" said Douglas, earnestly nodding his head. "You do keep the old place extremely well, I must say", the young man pronounced sincerely. He shook his head ruefully to convey his own impossibly awful deficiencies in the area of tidy housekeeping.

Isabel regarded her former lover disinterestedly. Yet it was always something of a wrench for her to note how Anna's beautiful green eyes were exactly the same shade as his. And even at the age of six, the little girl was already displaying something of her father's angular bearing – as well as his aptitude for taking centre stage by unconscious natural right, even with an audience of one.

Douglas Cameron was thirty-six, she knew, almost eight years older than herself. But with his long wavy hair, clear complexion, slightly exotic good looks and the vaguely ridiculous yet dashing eighteenth-century air which both attracted and amused his many lady friends, he might easily have passed for a man in his late twenties. The fact that he was also the father of a six-year-old girl – a status no attractive woman known to him for more than an hour or two was left unaware of – added to his obvious attractions an irresistible extra layer of life's heartwrenching glamour.

Regarding his lengthy affair with the child's mother, however, Douglas maintained a self-imposed silence that was full of agonised implication.

"Douglas", said Isabel carefully, "are you here for any particular purpose?"

"Purpose?" echoed Douglas in mock horror, resuming his seat. "Isabel my dear, a poet with a purpose is a contradiction in terms."

"I just thought", went on Isabel evenly, "that you might have wanted to apologise for not picking up Anna last Monday, like you were supposed to."

Douglas, still smiling, opened his eyes wide: "I left a message for you. Didn't you get it?"

"Yes. When I got back from working out of town, and after having Anna minded at short notice because you hadn't turned up – yes, I got your message."

"My shift was switched at the last minute", said Douglas, shrugging his shoulders. "You know what Carlton is like, wielding the sacred power recently entrusted to him: the Management of the Weekly Roster." Douglas inclined his body forward in mock reverence. "He likes to make sudden changes. I believe he's putting into practice the lessons he recently learned at a self-assertiveness course." The young man laughed brightly.

"Because you failed to turn up, I had to miss the early train, get the minder, pay her ten pounds that I can't afford and skip an appointment", said Isabel evenly.

Douglas had risen again and was closely examining a small woodframed Seurat print, one of only two adornments on the walls of the room. "That really is good", he pronounced emphatically, his back to Isabel. "The definition is dead on."

Vacantly, Isabel regarded his slim back, covered in a loose-fitting cashmere turtleneck sweater. His mop of shiny raven-black hair, which his girlfriends intuitively knew demanded regular rumpling, tumbled over the subdued red and grey stripes of a neat button-down shirt collar. His trousers were beige American chinos, cut in the generous fashion that would have looked wholly ridiculous on most men of his age, but which graced Douglas's figure to an extent Isabel found herself actually envying.

"Carlton's impossible", said Douglas suddenly, without turning from his examination of Isabel's only other framed print, a Dufy. "I had a regular shift – and despite what some people think I enjoy a regular way of life – and along comes Carlton to upset it. Now I'm getting stuck with these tedious shifts at the most awkward times." He shook his head to convey frustration.

Isabel was aware that is was quite unlike Douglas to emphasise an apology: so presumably the entire story was a fabrication. But dealing with an employee like Douglas could not be easy, for he did not need the job or the money.

Douglas Cameron had an independent allowance from his father, reputedly one of the country's wealthiest hop merchants, whom Douglas saw only very infrequently from his earliest years, and now hardly at all. John A. Cameron was simply a very busy man, yet he believed in fair dealing. Unable therefore to allot time to his only child, he had instead, from the very beginning, filled the gap with money. This followed naturally from the wealthy merchant's unoriginal but demonstrably accurate tenet (certainly in the hop trade) that time equalled money. The father saw very little of his son, but for the time denied, he conscientiously substituted money at the most generous hourly rates imaginable.

The end result was that – measured in cash terms, so to speak –

the young man's character now exhibited all the signs of an idyllic childhood.

"You writing much?" enquired Isabel idly.

"I'm working on a new collection" Douglas replied thoughtfully, switching from the frivolous tone he knew Isabel disliked.

"It's a single theme really, I've discovered – I didn't actually realise that myself for a while."

Douglas paused, but Isabel, recognising one of her former lover's characteristic gambits, chose to remain silent.

It really was time to begin thinking of a title for the collection, Douglas reminded himself. Titles were more important to the poetry-buying public than many people realised, and this new collection could be the one to copper-fasten his increasingly solid but still controversial reputation. And he had better also begin taking steps to ensure that when published, it did not fall into the wrong reviewing hands – he made a mental note to arrange an "accidental" meeting with the literary editor, who owed him a favour or two.

At any rate, a review such as the one which greeted his last volume, "One Sin Destroys a Sinner", was under no circumstances to be tolerated. The young man's nostrils flared angrily as he recalled yet again the insults, masquerading as literary criticism, proffered by that illiterate oaf Manningdale, who had christened him "a Phil Coulter of the canto, a Barry Manilow among bards."

"Rollicking Raoul", said Douglas after a brief pause, shaking his head and indicating the Duffy print. "I really enjoy that."

Douglas folded his arms and angled his head critically in front of the "Courses a Deauville". The picture's almost naive vivaciousness and its carefree, superficially slapdash use of primary colours rarely failed to amuse and intrigue the occasional visitor who inspected it; but is was a recognisably Douglas-Cameron gesture to admire something which he himself had presented as a gift.

"A happy man, but not a contented man – fortunately for him and for us", pronounced Douglas sententiously, nodding his head with carefully weighted appreciation.

Isabel was silent, recalling in still painful detail the day some seven years previously they had visited the National Gallery. Three months' pregnancy had raised only the gentlest abdominal curve, yet Douglas, the ecstatic father-to-be, had insisted on her wearing a billowing Laura Ashley smock which he himself had bought. "That's a dead giveaway" she had protested, laughing, but she had worn it to please him.

The riot of Duffy colour, the waves of unalloyed pleasure that emanated from the charmed visitors to the exhibition and the artist's own transparent delight in life's most accessible pleasures had uplifted them both to a state of near-euphoria.

Douglas had bought a mass of prints as they left, subsequently framing for her the one which now lit up her apartment wall. For a while there hung beside it the framed photograph he had taken the same day on the steps outside the gallery, using tripod and delayed shutter action to include himself in the photo, his arm around her, a cheeky finger pointing surreptitiously to the almost invisible bulge beneath the flowery smock. This picture Isabel had long put away, but the rectangular patch it once covered, beside the "Courses a Deauville" and less faded than the rest of the painted wall, was still a ghostly reminder.

"Can I see her?" enquired Douglas suddenly. Returning to perch on the edge of the armchair, he joined his elegant fingers together in front of his mouth as if praying. Swivelling the chair gently, he kept his green eyes fastened on Isabel's.

"For God's sake, Douglas, it's late – she's been asleep for ages." Irritation welled up in the child's mother.

Isabel stopped as abruptly as she had begun. She would remain calm. She had promised herself this from the moment of his arrival: she would stay in control.

Isabel no longer liked – did not retain the smallest shred of affection for – the man around whom her life had revolved for over three years. His poetry, which had once moved her young soul so passionately, now left her cold, even queasy, and in her heart she now agreed with those who found it saccharine, superficial and – ultimately – deeply dishonest.

Isabel now believed that work such as his reduced the creation of poetry to a playground where children like Douglas ran excitedly about, grabbing up indiscriminate, easily accessible handfuls of human emotion like so much wet sand. Out of this they constructed their elaborate, pretty castles of image, rhyme and metaphor, attached garish flags in the form of pretentious titles and vied bitterly, like all children, for the playground prize of public acclaim.

"Go ahead", she said quietly. "But please don't wake her."

Isabel's eyes travelled on to the Duffy, and she became suffused with a sort of lazy resignation, gradually transformed into pure pleasure as she saw the blue bird give way, almost merge with the blue cloud, and the vast scrummage of race spectators, packed shoulder to shoulder, joyfully follow the surging horses. A race on a clear day: even in the mere print, the harmony was palpable.

"She's amazing", breathed Douglas, emerging a little later from the bedroom. "Amazing."

"You didn't wake her?" questioned Isabel automatically.

"No, no."

Isabel regarded Douglas coldly again. He could not make himself available as arranged on a morning when Anna was fractious, irritable, grubby and unpleasant, and he had thrown her own arrangements into disarray. But he could breeze in uninvited at a late hour and admire the sleeping angel.

Douglas now proceeded to dart about the room, touching, inspecting. Isabel felt a renewed rush of irritation – the man was like a bloody detective looking for clues and fingerprints. One might have thought he had never before been in the apartment, when he had actually lived there with her for a year and a half.

Douglas paused at the back of the chair over which Isabel had laid her clothes. He fingered the well-cut skirt, another of his presents to her, and the cool lace blouse. Then he picked up the blue satin bra and regarded it quizzically, with the interest a policeman with a passion for detail might bestow on a suspect driving licence.

Isabel flushed with anger and embarrassment as she saw Douglas gently caress the silky garment, peering intently at one of its sheer half-spheres as if it were a crystal ball about to reveal life's secrets.

"Douglas", she said, controlling her voice with difficulty, "It's late. I have to get up early tomorrow and I want to go to bed."

Douglas started mildly and an attractive mischievous smile graced his features. As he laid down the bra, Isabel's angry eyes caught him dart a glance at the bedroom. With the door left half-open, a corner of the double bed with its dark blue coverlet over the plump pink duvet was clearly visible.

"On my own" said Isabel thickly.

Douglas grinned. "Never mind", he said brightly. "Anyway, strictly speaking I've sworn off all that sort of thing for a month. I just thought, perhaps for old times' sake?"

"Especially not for old times' sake", said Isabel quietly.

"Well, I really must be off" said Douglas, displaying his facility for intimating that he was being detained against his will.

"Don't forget about Anna on Saturday", replied Isabel, taking his coat from the hanger.

Douglas was momentarily taken aback. "Oh yes, yes. I'm looking forward to that. Going to take her somewhere special – I haven't quite decided yet."

"I wish you wouldn't", said Isabel coldly.

Douglas moved to the door, tying the wide belt of the flowing tweed coat in a loose knot. Stopping abruptly, he cocked his ear carefully as the subdued music playing on the Akai penetrated his consciousness for the first time.

"Ah. Sibelius."

Isabel felt a pang of annoyance and disappointment at not having recognised earlier the music of her favourite composer. It was doubly irritating that Douglas should seize on it.

"The Second Symphony", mused the young poet. "Personally, I much prefer the Fifth." Douglas felt he should be something of a populist these days – the times through which he was living seemed to demand it of him.

"Drink problem of course", he mused wickedly, his hand on the doorknob. "That's the price you pay for being Finnish." He laughed: "Did you know he destroyed his last work – what was going to be the Eighth Symphony?" Isabel did know it. She kept silent.

"Burnt it", said Douglas cheerfully. "In his house." He laughed again. Flashing a broad smile, he opened the door and departed without saying goodbye.

Seating herself stiffly at the kitchen table, Isabel swallowed the cold dregs of the coffee. She was shivering, and close to tears.

Pressed rigidly against the back of the chair where her clothes hung, she sat staring at the closed door for fully twenty minutes. Gradually, she became conscious of a hard bulge pressing into her back. She rose, picked up her skirt, put her hand in the deep pocket and took out a crisp new packaged wad of five-pound notes. She did not need to count them: stamped on the tight beige paper band was "£40".

Isabel flushed with anger. This was her former boyfriend's puerile way of handing over what was legally hers – and only a small part of what was rightly hers – as if it were a secret generous gift.

Still shivering, she sat down again and pressed the play button on the Akai. The tape had rewound itself and soon the restrained, holy quietism of the symphony was permeating the room, its intricate harmonies gradually possessing and calming the woman's soul. And then Isabel realised, with only the smallest sense of satisfaction, that Douglas was wrong. It was not the Second Symphony, but the Sixth.

Slowly, Isabel relaxed and was drawn into the serene, sad intimacies. Without rancour, she recalled the young poet's jibe at the final musical work of the aged composer. Because it did not live up to his own aspirations, the old man had consigned to the flames the symphony which might have given some easy pleasure, and perhaps a great deal more, to thousands of those who loved him then and now.

Isabel felt she knew exactly how Douglas would argue the case. To people like him, such a wilful act of destruction was clear proof of senile dementia – exacerbated for Sibelius by his problems with alcohol: because if a publisher was willing to accept work from an established artist, print it and pay for it, then only a fool would walk away. Either that, or the man was suffused with an outrageous degree of pride.

Too damned weird and wonderful for the world to appreciate would summarise the composer's attitude to his work, as attributed to Douglas. If the notion of humility occurred to him, Douglas might not immediately scorn it, but he would argue that high self-esteem was a pre-requisite for the success of the creatively talented, and it was of the utmost importance not to let the certainty of one's own worth be undervalued or diminished in any way. One must therefore assume that herein lay the old composer's regrettable error. And Isabel could without difficulty imagine Douglas jostling to be the first in the queue to forgive him.

A fragment of something she had once read – a letter, she recalled, written by Sibelius's wife of more than fifty years, imploded in Isabel's bludgeoned consciousness: "There was a big bonfire here, but I stayed in another room."

A low moan brought Isabel to her feet. She moved quickly and silently to the bedroom to comfort the still sleeping child, momentarily disturbed by some transient phantasm of an unknown dream. Isabel sat on the bed, from where she could see the flames of the dying fire throw flickering shadows through her silent living-room. Around the motionless woman, the music surged and flowed like a rushing brook.